The Watching

The Watching

DANÉ AND JULIE LE ROUX

iUniverse, Inc.
Bloomington

The Watching

iUniverse books may be ordered through booksellers or by contacting:

iUniverse
1663 Liberty Drive
Bloomington, IN 47403
www.iuniverse.com
1-800-Authors (1-800-288-4677)

ISBN: 978-1-4620-3859-6 (sc)
ISBN: 978-1-4620-3991-3 (ebk)

Printed in the United States of America

iUniverse rev. date: 03/13/2012

It all started on September 22, 2009.

But that wasn't where it all began.

Chapter 1

The sky was lit by the full moon shining through the dark clouds but with an odd atmosphere; it was still dark and creepy. I personally wanted to go home, but Suria suggested earlier that we go to the Beautiful Blue, a nearby creek that the town thought was haunted, and sadly I accepted. At first I thought it was a joke and we weren't really going searching for a ghost; I was distracted by her long blonde hair shining brightly against the moon's light.

I sat patiently in the passenger seat of my car and watched as the road under us disappeared. I was often nervous, and I let Suria drive my car to the Blue, but I also knew that if I drove, I wouldn't have gotten much farther than the driveway itself. I disliked driving at night.

The Beautiful Blue ran through a clearing that consisted of a big, flat field that was surrounded by tall pine trees. The creek itself was located on the farthest end of the field from the entrance to the clearing, also bordered by a line of tall cypress trees. To get to the Blue was the easy bit; the parking lot was not far from the little trail that went through the trees, and the trail had a few turns but eventually came out into the clearing. The Blue was a rather secret place because newcomers didn't know how to get there, if they even knew about it at all. It was the usual hangout for the teenagers of Ellsberg. Near the creek was a big hill, and on that hill was an old building known as Mr. Funke's Hot Springs.

The Hot Springs sold hot tubs and would have at least three hot tubs going during the winter for people to use for just recreational purposes. This guy was really in the money.

"Let's go, we have school tomorrow," I said as I turned my head from the window to look at her, but Suria's determination was set.

"Come on, Marissa, have some excitement in your life. You're too scared to try new things." She peered over the steering wheel, making sure she was still on the road and not in the ditch.

"I have enough excitement in my life; I just don't want to go in the dark," I told her as I watched her slowly park the car. "And it's not like I'm scared to try new things, I just would rather try something that involved daytime."

I reluctantly followed her as she climbed out of the car. The grass was still wet from the rain that had fallen that morning, and I felt my shoes soaking up the leftover water on the tar. I looked around before I began to walk onto the trail to the creek; the darkness made it hard to see beneath our feet. Suria seemed to not notice my nervousness about the darkness, probably because the trees on the path had blocked out any light from the moon.

"Hurry," she yelled, looking back at me to make sure I was still there. "I want to see if it is true. That creepy old man said that there was something hiding in the Blue at night."

I didn't like this idea, not one bit. Who in her right mind would want to go looking for something at night? It was obviously hidden for a reason, and I wanted to take no part in it.

As we carried on, I made sure to not glance around at my surrounding for things that could possibly turn into something scary. I kept my focus on the ground ahead of me because I knew my imagination would go wild if I stared into the shadows that lay just between the trees. I grabbed my black hair nervously and started to twist a strand around my finger. I was scared of the dark—I know that's sad for a 16-year-old, but I always liked to know where I was going and to not worry about the shadows that overtook the night. I looked up so I could see the little bit of light from the moon, but it didn't make me feel better because the clouds looked mysterious and dangerous, two words I didn't like to use in the same sentence.

"I've heard rumours," Suria told me as she quickened her pace. I tried to keep up, my steps falling into rhythm behind her. I knew we were getting closer to the creek when I could faintly hear the rush of water.

"Let's head back; we can come here any other day," I suggested to her.

Suria glanced back at me. "We are here already, so we might as well see if what he said was true."

We finally came upon the Blue, and I stared straight at the trees around the creek. It was really a pretty place—in the daytime, that was. Neither of us had been here at nighttime; no one dared to because an old man in the town said something lived here, and when someone said something creepy, everyone tended to believe it.

I looked around at the empty field that lay ahead of me, and Suria moved herself more into the clearing, taking small yet careful steps. The moon now appeared out of the clouds, regaining its peaceful state and showing me that there was nothing to be afraid of.

"Come on, Suria, we are here … now let's head back," I said as I walked up to join her. We both searched the area around us, but even with the moon's light it was hard to see the picnic benches that were only metres away from us.

She looked at me and smiled. "You're such a coward," she joked, and then she pointed across the creek. "I don't think we'll see anything in the field, but if we head across the creek and into the trees, then maybe something is hiding in there."

"Really? You want to go toward the trees that we can barely see into? Well doesn't that sound like a really smart idea," I pointed out sarcastically.

She gave me one last glare before she headed toward the bridge. We walked along the creek; the water was soothing, and the moonlight reflecting off the water made it easier to find the bridge. I let Suria lead us over the dark wooden bridge. I wasn't too sure why there was a bridge that led us just into trees, but maybe there was a path that none of us knew about that would lead us to the Hot Springs. We carried on, and the deeper we went, the thicker the trees became. I stepped over a few fallen trunks. It seemed now that the trees were overtaking us, and we had to watch where we stepped.

Ten minutes went by and nothing happened. "See anything?" I asked her.

"No," she said sadly.

"I guess rumours are just rumours." I tried to cheer her up, but I could tell that she was still disappointed having not seen anything.

"Come on, Marissa, let's go." She realized she had brought me here for nothing.

We turned around, and I led us back over the bridge. When I took my first step on the bridge, I felt the entire atmosphere around us change, like someone else was now with us, like someone else was watching us. A sudden chill ran up my spine. I turned to look at Suria, who now stood completely still; I could tell she had felt it too because she looked behind her nervously and then started to search all around us.

"Can you feel that?" she asked. I slowly nodded my head. Something had changed, and I was scared to look behind me toward the clearing. The creek became lighter, and now I saw all around me as if it were daytime. I looked up to see if the moon was providing all the light, but the clouds hid the full moon perfectly, which meant that something else was providing the extra light.

For a moment it was very calm and quiet, and I tried to listen for the creek's water or even a cricket chirping. Our surroundings seemed to have paused, with time frozen completely. Then all at once it was shattered by a twig being snapped.

"What was that?" Suria whispered to me. I couldn't answer her—I was too scared. I could feel my heart beat faster in my chest, and I held my breath as if to help make myself invisible. My eyes grew wider as I looked to see who was there. Another twig snapped; the noise came from behind Suria and in the trees. Her eyes told me that she was scared. I turned around to look back onto the field to see if she had seen anything behind me, but there was nothing. Another twig snapped, but this time it felt like it was all around us. Another branch broke, this time in the opposite direction.

I stole another glance at Suria, but she faced away from me and looked toward the trees. I could tell she hadn't heard the noise, and I squinted trying to see better. The creek was still dark from the shadows the moon had created. I looked at every tree individually to make sure nothing was out of place. The creek's rushing water had splashed up near the ridges of the banks where I stood. Another tree branch broke, this time right behind me. I took two closer steps to Suria. I was now off the bridge and could feel the moist ground under me. She still faced away from me, and I wanted her to look at me, but my body seemed to have frozen in its spot. The air was thick and smoky, making it difficult to breathe.

It grew to an awkward silence as we waited for another sound, and I looked in Suria's direction one more time before I turned my head so that I could find the exit to the Blue. I looked back at Suria, who now turned her head to face me. I stared at her face and couldn't help but imagine that the 'shadows that the moon had created were evil creatures.'

In the distance I could hear owls making their hooting cries. It was like they didn't know the other part of a knock-knock joke. Someone had to teach them the other half of the joke.

Suria whispered louder now. "Let's go."

My feet started to make their way back where they had came from, and I felt for the wooden bridge with my foot. Snap! My body froze; another branch had broken, and this time it was a bigger one. It came from behind us—or maybe in front of us; it was hard to tell. I stood still as movement occurred around me, and I saw that Suria's feet had inched back a bit. I slowly turned my head so I could take a quick glance around me, but instead I focused on Suria's face. I winced when her eyes showed me that there was something behind me, and she seemed as if she was about to cry. *Now who's the scared one?* I thought, but then realized I was too scared to even display any sort of emotion on my own face. The forest lightened up even more, and the shadows were fading. Her body tensed, and I couldn't help but take a look at what was behind me.

Across the bridge from me was … nothing. I looked back at her to see if she still stared behind me but now she faced the other direction again toward the dark trees to the far left. Her light-coloured hair didn't move with the wind. It was times like these I was happy my hair was black and shoulder length; it made it harder to see me, camouflaging me in the night—but I guessed it wouldn't help if I had been spotted already.

I turned around and saw nothing, and I could feel myself begin to relax until branches snapped in every direction. We still had not moved from where we stood, waiting again for another sound. After half a minute of no sounds, I began to feel the tension loosen from the air, and we both started to relax. Suria took another step closer to me as well as the water.

We stood there for a few more moments, and I had hoped that by now we would be back in the car and away from the trees. At the least we should have put more distance between us and the water—and whatever was lurking out there. I began to fiddle with my hair, twirling it around my finger.

Suria blinked.

"Do you see anything?" I asked. She looked at me and shook her head. My mind started to play tricks on me. It was like when someone stared at a spot for too long, and everything seemed to blur together. The forest ahead of me didn't look like trees and shrubs that were green and had little bugs in them; now that the source of light was fading, they started to look creepy, like their only purpose was to eventually take me down. I feared to have to walk through them to get back to safety.

Something was out of place, and it grabbed my attention instantly. I began to see a figure in the forest behind Suria—not a human figure. Suria's hand, which felt icy cold, grabbed my arm, and shivers ran up my spine. My eyes started to adjust to the figure the more I focused on it. At first it looked like mist, a slow fog in the distance, but it soon began to grow a faint outline of a … wolf?

My reflexes kicked in, and I started to move away from the wolf. A high squeal escaped my mouth, and Suria looked at me and then turned to see what was behind her. Her hair covered her face as the wind grew stronger each second. I looked back at the wolf, and its body was clearer and more defined. It was large but still not realistic, and if I looked carefully, I would be able to see the bushes straight behind it. I felt my feet near the edge of the bank, just barely on the bridge. I was surprised that this wooden plank was even considered a bridge. Suria took a few steps back, and I had to glance down to make sure I wouldn't fall over anything.

"What do we do?" she whispered.

"Well, let's try to slowly make our way around it and back to the car, or at least away from the forest," I said, and then I realized the wolf was gone. My heart jumped from my chest as I stared into the dark forest. "Where is it?"

Suria looked back and then shrugged and she began to slowly move away from where the wolf had once stood only metres from her. The feeling I got earlier was still present, the eerie sense that something was watching us. I assumed it was the wolf, but a wolf couldn't possibly be see-through. It must have been only a bit of fog, and I was just being a scaredy-cat, as usual.

I blinked, and a large white object flashed before me. I backed up to escape from it, but I had no idea where the bridge had gone because nothing supported my weight anymore. Everything went dark and cold.

Chapter 2

I sank like a rock, but I didn't hit the bottom. Water rushed over me and under me, and I could feel myself being taking away by the current, which was cold and made my body numb. Everything around me was dark, as if I were being swallowed by the cold night.

I kicked and swung my arms, hoping to reach the surface, but my attempts seemed like they were getting me nowhere, and I was frightened instantly. A scream left my throat, but I just watched as little bubbles floated to the surface. I was going to die! I tried to move myself again, but it felt like something or someone was weighing me down and holding me under the water. For a brief moment, something grabbed onto my ankles but let go instantly. A boost of energy ran throughout my body, and I moved my arms quickly.

Air greeted me as I reached the surface after many struggles. I sucked in a huge gasp and felt my lungs happily take in air. I struggled to find a bank or anything to grab on to and pull myself out of the water. I was a lot colder now that I was drenched. I noticed that I had been taken quite far from the bridge, but luckily I was closer to the ground that was by the field and not the forest. I pulled myself up on the shoreline so I wasn't in the cold water anymore, but my clothes were still wet and cold, and my body began to shake uncontrollably. My feet were still in the water, but I couldn't find the strength to pull them out. I searched the area: the shadows from the moon danced—and they looked like small, evil beings.

I searched around anxiously for Suria. I looked up at the bridge to see if she still stood there, but she was gone. I hoped I hadn't taken her into the water with me. I heard faint coughing come from farther down the creek from me. My head turned automatically to the sound. Suria hung onto the bank , and I slowly climbed out farther from the water to help her. For a few seconds I crawled on the ground, scared I would be thrown back into the water.

Once I was far enough to stand, I checked to make sure she still clung to the edge. I was lucky enough to get an easy shoreline so that I could hoist my body out. Once my feet were steady and balanced, I ran to Suria, grabbed her hands, and helped pull her from the water. Suria continued coughing; I gave her a few seconds to gather some air as I looked back at the forest and across the creek for the wolf. Hidden in the darkness between two trees was a pair of green eyes piercing through the heavy fog, and a low snarl echoed through the air.

Her eyes opened. "Are you okay?" I yelled at her. "Get up!"

I didn't give her time to respond and quickly grabbed her arm and pulled her to her feet. My hair dripped onto my shoulders and back, and the water running down my back felt extremely uncomfortable. Suria coughed a little more before she began to run. What had just happened? It was reasons like this I was terrified of the dark; things always wanted to hide in it, and not being able to see those things was the worse bit, especially if they could see me.

I didn't have time for second thoughts; now that we had started to move it seemed to have set off a chain reaction in the Beautiful Blue. I pushed countless branches out of my way, but I was too cold to take complete notice. It was everywhere, completely surrounding us, and I soon heard sounds of quick footsteps running in the forest. I flinched at the snapping of branches coming from every direction possible. I glanced behind at Suria; her face held no emotion, and she too looked back to see if the fog was still there. I focused on the entrance, but Suria seemed to have gained some adrenaline and ran ahead of me.

I made sure I stayed close behind Suria as she ran, but when she was scared she could run faster than I could. We ran across the field easily and only took a few seconds to find the entrance to the trail to the parking lot. She didn't notice, but every time she would push away a branch for herself, it'd end up hitting me in the face. I tripped over and over again as I ran.

Surprisingly, she hadn't gotten very far ahead of me, and I caught up to her. The trail felt never-ending, and for a moment I thought we would never get off of it. I looked down and saw that there was a tree stump, and I took one gallant leap over it and landed in the street. I gasped hard from everything that had just happened. The branches continued to snap and break behind us. Suria sounded short of breath as well, but when I saw that we were finally away from the Blue, I felt victory explode through my veins. We made it!

The air was humid now, and the clouds hid the full moon again. Now I had to use the streetlights for guidance, but any light other than the moon was fine by me. My hands rested on my knees as I tried getting more air into my lungs. I stared at the ground and wanted to sleep on it, longing for this all just to end. I was exhausted. My clothes grew colder and now clung against my body. No cars were in sight, and the street lay still and empty. I heard Suria panting.

"Let's go," I said again to Suria. I looked up at her and saw that she was staring back toward the trees. I took her arm and tried to pull her away from the trail, away from the trees and the Blue.

She resisted. "Look," she whispered.

I stopped and looked back at the trees.

At first I saw the ordinary trees, but then my eyes widened once I saw what she had noticed, and it took me a while to actually figure out what it was. A faint mist had outlined the shape of a huge dog that stood on the border of the woods, and it seemed to light up the area around it. The eyes watched us intently; I figured that this mist was what had provided the light beforehand, back by the bridge. I took a step back and tried to make myself as quiet and unnoticeable as I could because I didn't want to set this thing off and make it attack us. My plan was to very slowly back away with as little movement as possible. I was right with my first guess earlier: it was a large wolf, bigger than any other I had ever seen. It actually seemed unnaturally big—but then again, it also didn't seem to have a solid body, as if were made out of thick, foggy air. Its large white paw moved forward and stopped. The wolf's head hung low.

I took a quick glance toward Suria; she hadn't said much since the creek and just stood completely frozen, glaring at the mist creature. Her eyes were wide with fear. *We need to get out of here*, I thought. I looked at the car and then back toward Suria, who stood between me and the wolf. What if it tried to hurt us—or worse, kill us? Suria turned away from me and looked back at the wolf, and it had moved itself a few steps closer to us, which set me off.

My instincts kicked in once again, and I figured this mist must be the reason I had fallen into the creek and almost died. What if that was its plan—to lure us in? Though that didn't make any sense—it was only fog, right? I quickly glanced back at the wolf, and it took another step closer to Suria. I saw almost every detail on it: the wolf had large green eyes that sparkled extremely bright. Was it trying to blind us now? It was like a large dog of some sort, but I was surprised I had not noticed the eyes first, which shined more brightly than when a flashlight was shined on a cat's eyes at night. I could see the faint outline of the trees directly behind the creature. The wolf took another step closer, which let me get a better look at it. I could see that it was there, but at the same time I could see right through it. The wolf's eyes were a vibrant green color, and it looked like it was about to take another step toward us, slowly creeping closer.

"Run!" I yelled. Not only did I yell it at Suria, but I yelled it to myself. My feet felt locked to the ground and needed help to move from their spot. When I started to run to my car, I pretty much ran on Jell-O legs but managed to stay ahead of Suria. I was lucky that it had rained the day before because I could hear her steps behind me and wouldn't have to check to see if she was still there. I feared something would happen to us.

"Suria! Car keys, please!" I yelled at her; this time I was going to drive. In a half daze she threw me the car keys, and I fumbled with them. I looked up to make sure the mist had not run after us, but it was gone. Suria stood next to my car and stared back at where the wolf was. Would she rather look at that thing than get into the car? What if it tried to kill us? Fear washed over me from head to toe.

"Marissa, what was that?" she asked. Like I would know. I grunted. "It was such a soothing sound. I would love to hear it again. It was something I've never heard before. Did you hear the humming?"

My heart stopped when she asked that last question because I had not heard any sound from the wolf. Was I missing something? Her brown eyes blazed at me for an answer. I didn't know what to say; did I just miss the sound because I was too scared, or was she making this up?

"Suria, what sound? I didn't hear anything," I said as I unlocked the car door.

Her mouth pulled together, forming thin lips, and she looked like she was trying really hard to hold back tears. "The humming! It came from that thing, and the song calmed me down a lot. I wasn't even scared anymore. I think I may have even heard that sound before." She paused before speaking again. "It was so different, so pretty. Did you really not hear it?" She quickly got into the car and looked back once more at the woods. I slowly drove it farther and farther from the Blue.

"Next time you want to do something creepy, ask someone else," I told her, and she looked at me understandingly. "That thing tried to kill us. I think I actually stopped breathing!"

Why did she always want to do something insane? I wasn't angry with her; I was just overwhelmed with what had happened. I looked at Suria to make sure I had not hurt her feelings. She looked really sad, and I really didn't want to say anything else in case I made things worse.

"I'm sorry," I said, and she looked at me strangely. "I just … don't like those kinds of things."

"No, it's okay, I just wish you heard the humming," she said sadly again and turned her head away to look back out of the window. Shouldn't she be a bit happy? We saw something out of the ordinary! Usually that would have excited her.

I drove her home and got out to give her a quick hug good-bye. She seemed better as I watched her open the front door to her house. I hoped her parents weren't too mad that she was a few hours past curfew, but they were easygoing. Once she entered the house, I sat back in the car. I knew that tomorrow I would be picking up Suria for school in the morning like usual. Her birthday was late in the year, and she wouldn't be getting her license anytime soon. Suria and I had been best friends for five years, since she had moved to Ellsberg when the Andersons adopted her. Suria never liked to speak about her past, and I never pushed her to say any more than she wanted to.

As I drove I started to replay the night in my head over and over again, and I wondered if maybe there was a reason it hadn't hurt us. If it had attacked us, would we be able to feel it? Was it really made out of fog? That was impossible. But then why did it look like it was?

I parked the car in the driveway to my house and stared at the front door, knowing I would have to enter it sooner or later. The lawn had two large hedges on either side that hid most of the stairs that led to the porch. It was an average-looking brick house, very modern and typical, and the stairs were a dark brick that led to a rather small white patio porch. On the far end were two white chairs. The grass on the front lawn was tall and reminded me of when I was little: I would run through the grass because I thought I was invisible. At times like this, I really wished I was. I sighed and trudged myself up to the doorway, preparing myself to face my mom because of how I looked. The creature entered in and out of my mind, and I kept wondering what it wanted. A cold shiver ran down my back, and I had an eerie sense that I was not alone again. My clothes were still damp, which made every little wind feel like it went right through my skin and into my bones.

My mind flashed back to the wolf, which had been made of a mist that seemed to shine and form around it. The wolf had been an odd white color, and its green eyes, the greenest color I had ever seen, were very bright.

Just before I entered the door, I looked over my shoulder to make sure that no one was behind me, but all I saw was the two streetlights that stood tall on either side of the street and captured the darkness. Unfortunately it didn't capture or hide *all* darkness.

The doorknob squeaked as I turned it, and my feet felt like they weighed down every part of my body. I took one last look at the sky, and it danced with lights—airplanes and satellites that moved and manoeuvred themselves around the stars without a problem. It seemed as though every moment they were in the sky they would make it a memorable one. I opened the door and walked in.

My family was waiting up for me. A quick flash of the mist ran through my mind again, and I tried to shake it away. I wanted the mist to run away to the stars to join the dance with the satellites and spaceships. I smiled and wondered again what it was like up there, but my smile faded once I heard a voice yell my name.

"Marissa!" My mom came from the kitchen. "Where have you been? You're two hours past your curfew." She took a good look at me. "And what happened to you! Explain yourself."

I needed to think of an excuse and needed it quick, but my mind went completely blank, and I wished I had come up with some sort of excuse in the car, something to tell her that sounded reasonable. I could tell her I ran into a tree, but all I could think about was the mist wolf. I closed my eyes for a few seconds. I could still feel my mom gazing down at me; I hated when she did that. She had this certain look that made me reveal all my secrets.

"Suria forgot to turn off her sprinklers," I told her, but even fighting a tree was more believable than sprinklers going off at midnight. I looked at her and could tell that she didn't buy my story. I smiled pathetically at her as she stood with her hands on her hips. The cream colors from the walls brought out the pink in her silk pyjamas. Her dark brown hair lay straight on her shoulders, just like mine. Her large blue eyes stared into mine as she searched for the truth, and I made sure that my eyes didn't give it away. Then she gave me one more overall look at my damp body, wet hair, and dirty clothes. Mom pushed her hair off her shoulders.

"Sprinklers, eh?" One eyebrow lifted. "Go get yourself cleaned up before you get a cold, and put those filthy clothes in the washer. Please and thank you, Hun." She promptly turned around and headed back into the kitchen. Well, that was a freebee, because I could tell that she didn't believe me, but I had gotten away with it. She'd just think I was crazy if I told her I had seen a ghost—or was it even a ghost?

The door to my house led straight to the TV room and a hallway to the kitchen, and by the TV room was a staircase upstairs to a spare bedroom, my parents' bedroom, and a bathroom. I led myself down the hallway to the kitchen. The kitchen walls were a dark orange with black tiles and countertops. It reminded me of one of the times Suria had come over. It was a boiling hot day, so we decided to just lie on the tiles and talk. I told her about my life, and she shared what she could remember of her childhood before she was turned into an Anderson. We decided that day that we would make up tons of memories for her.

I quickly gave my dad a nod of greeting and went downstairs. The wall paint in the basement had been chosen by my brother, Daniel, and me. Daniel was on the couch; he looked away from me. His hair stood high and spiked up. "Hey," he said and then looked back at the clock on the wall. "You're home pretty late; where were you?"

"I was with Suria," I told him as I made my way to my room.

"Your clothes are wet," he pointed out, and I just nodded before I shut my room door behind me.

I didn't like the feeling of wet clothes that clung as close to the skin as possible. I quickly took them off and then grabbed a towel for the hot bath that I drew. I climbed into the tub. The hot water gave my toes a slight tingling feeling, and soon my entire body burned from the sensation. My dad once told me that the best thoughts were done in the bathtub, and he was right; it was quiet and peaceful.

What had happened today? Had we simply imagined everything? But Suria and I both saw this mist-like, creature-wolf thing. My mind hurt. It was also possible that our minds had played a trick on us because once you believe you see something, the power of the mind would eventually make one see it. We'd barely had any light, and it had been completely dark. The green eyes could easily have been some sort of bug. But I knew deep down that what we had seen tonight had happened—and what about the twigs breaking? It would have been impossible for someone to have snapped all those branches so quickly. I got out of the bath and trudged slowly to my bed.

I watched the shadows on my walls created by my lava lamp; they ran across the walls, and I couldn't help but picture that they were playing a game of hide-and-go-seek. *Hide, little ones, hide!* I thought. This was a lot easier to fall asleep to than counting sheep.

Did Suria say she heard humming? I sure hadn't heard any humming. Maybe she was crazier than me. This thought somewhat satisfied me.

I wanted to know a lot more about this creature. For some odd reason, I was very fascinated by it, and this was odd for someone who was afraid of everything. But for all I knew, I was a crazy science freak. I grabbed my sheets and crawled into bed. I soon fell asleep cheering for the shadows.

Chapter 3

I thought about my dream as I got ready for school. I dreamed that the mist creature was circling us in the clearing, and it seemed to eye Suria like a piece of meat. Its eyes shone bright green like they had before, and every few seconds it would get closer and closer. I woke up before it got within reach of Suria. In a way I was relieved that I'd had this dream because it was the first time in a long time that I had dreamed of anything other than my usual ones. Was this dream a sign? No, it couldn't be—but I usually dreamed of nothing, and if not nothing, that nightmare— so this was one of my normal dreams. Is that why I thought it was a sign? My phone rang, and I ran across my room to answer it.

"Hello?" I said.

"Hey, it's me, Suria! I'm wondering if you're picking me up today."

"Yeah I am, usual time," I said as I looked into the mirror.

"Okay, 'bye."

I hung up the phone and continued to get ready. I started to do my hair in ringlets, and I put a small blue clip in my hair to complete it. I exhaled and slid my phone into my pocket while I finished getting ready. I headed out the front door to my car, and when I looked around I saw that Daniel had already left for school in his red Jeep, and my parents had left for work early.

One question ran through my head as I started up my car: What did this creature want? I drove silently down the street completely lost in thought. The roads were empty except for random people headed for school, and in the distance I saw Suria standing on her front lawn waiting for me. Her house was also modern except for the one lonely shrub that sat in her yard and the bright red window panels. When she first moved to Ellsberg, we had this game where we would hide behind the shrub and watch cars drive by in the hopes that they wouldn't see us, but we got too big and bored to hide behind a bush all day, and that's when we discovered the Beautiful Blue.

She jumped into my car as I parked.

"Hey," she muttered under her breath.

"Hello," I responded as a reflex, and then I asked, "How did you sleep?" Did she dream too? I looked back at her.

"I slept fine." As I pulled out of the driveway, I heard her say quietly, "I don't think it's after us."

"What makes you say that?" I asked.

"I don't have any real proof of that, but don't you think it would have done something if it was going to hurt us?"

"Maybe it was waiting for the perfect time."

"Is it even a real thing? Like a ghost or something?" she asked.

I shrugged as I turned into the school parking lot. I parked in front of the school, and she looked at me carefully.

"You get out, and I'll park the car," I explained.

She didn't argue as she gathered her stuff up and got out. I sat and fortunally there was an open parking spot. *I'd better not be late*, I thought. Eventually I saw a grade twelve student arriving at the same time. I took his space, gathered all my books and binders, and then dragged myself from the car toward the big yellow entrance doors.

Once I entered the hallways, I walked down my brother Daniel's hall. He was leaning up against the wall, and it looked as though he was trying to get Suria's attention as she spoke to a friend next to him. I slid myself beside her.

"Hey, guys," I said, greeting the crowd. I looked at Daniel, who still gawked at Suria. He had liked her since the first day he had laid eyes on her, and I couldn't blame him because a good dose of the guys in the school had little crushes on her at one point or another. Daniel was the one who never quite stopped loving and in it was a bit humorous, mostly because Suria loved to tease the poor kid. He was two years older than me and three years older than Suria. Daniel and his 18-year-old buddies were riots, or so they thought. I left Suria and Daniel and headed to class, and then I heard my name being called from behind.

"Marissa! Marissa!" I turned around to see Kim, her dark red curly hair almost covering her face.

I gently smiled at her. "Hey Kim, what's happening?"

Her pace fell in step with mine as I continued to walk to my class. "It's the annual Hot Springs Dumping today; did you forget? I hear it's the biggest group yet. Are you in?" she asked nicely. Her red hair bounced as she spoke.

"Of course, I go every year." I felt a little bad that I had forgotten about it. "Thanks for reminding me, by the way." I nodded my head with a soft smile, and then the bell rang and I entered my class. I tried my best to find a seat in the very back row, but no such luck. I had to settle for the second row from the back, and Kim took a seat next to me.

"I can't believe that you forgot!" she exclaimed. I gave her an apologetic smile and watched as our teacher, Mr. Robituson, entered the class. For some reason he always wore a lab coat to class, and no one knew why. Did he honestly think that some kids would try to blow up their math assignments? (Well, who was I kidding—some kids would love to.) I honestly thought he was crazy, but in a good sense because even if I tried, I couldn't think of one kid in the entire school who didn't like Mr. Robituson. He could make Abraham Lincoln and Mona Lisa crack up, he was so funny. I started to bite my nails, a habit I have been trying to break for years.

Kim's eyes lit up from behind her glasses. "Great, don't forget your swimsuit." I nodded my head and gave her another smile. Mr. Robituson greeted us with a short wave and then proceeded to his desk. He had very narrow glasses that hung on the end of his nose, and he always looked around to stare at the kids before class started. I remembered how he would ask really stupid questions on our tests. One question was what should he have for supper, and one of the answers a kid gave was "your lab coat." But I couldn't imagine him eating his lab coat because he would cry about it and then have to go buy another one.

I looked around to see who was near me. Britney was on the other side of me, and beside her was her boyfriend, Josh. Britney's hair was very straight, shiny black, and extremely long. Josh had really blonde spiky hair, and a few freckles covered his face. Britney's giggles interrupted my thoughts as I watched her and Josh write love notes to each other. I felt sick. Sometimes I thought that they only came to school to flirt.

"Kids," announced Mr. Robituson, "I have an announcement!" No one heard him over all the chattering. "Hello!" he hollered, and there was instant silence. "That's better. Now, do you remember me saying that we are getting a new student? Well, I didn't lie. Everybody, this is William Carrington. Come on in, William."

A tall, good-looking boy entered the classroom; he looked at us very shyly and gave a greeting nod. His green eyes looked around again, and he then proceeded to pick up his binder and walk to an empty seat across the room from me. I noticed all the girls stealing glances at the new kid. I was relieved that Suria wasn't in this class because she would have stolen his heart instantly. But sadly I knew that they would eventually encounter each other.

"He is really something, eh? I'm going to invite him to the Big Blue tonight," Kim whispered to me with a slight giggle. I smiled at her comment like I always did and looked back at William, but he seemed so far away now.

As class progressed, I looked for the millionth time in the direction of Will, and to my surprise he looked back at me. His vibrant eyes met with mine, and I felt my face turn red; he had seen me look at him! I hoped he didn't think it was weird of me for staring at him, but I took a quick glance around the rest of the room and saw that other girls also stared at him. I didn't want to be just one of the girls who stared at the new kid, so I instantly turned away and stared out the window.

I waited silently for the bell to ring so I could quietly make a quick escape from Will, and I began to wonder why it always felt like time slowed down when I wanted it to fly by. Finally the little ding went off, and I quickly grabbed my textbook and ran to the door. When I reached the door, I looked to my left to see Will just inches from me. I gave him a shy smile when he noticed me.

I started off with, "Hello, my name is—" but I got cut off when the other girls had caught up to him too, wanting to introduce themselves. I manoeuvred myself around them and broke free for the hallway. My thoughts seemed to be erased of Will when my dream entered my mind again, and I thought back to my usual nightmare that stirred my sleep every night. Last night's was nothing compared to my nightmare. I looked back at Will, who was surrounded by the girls; he seemed to be like the new candy in a sweet shop.

I walked to my next class, which was with Suria. I sat next to her, and she immediately began to talk. "Weird things have happened to me since last night," she whispered to me.

"Like what?"

"It's like I'm never alone anymore. I don't know, it's just a weird thing. Sorry I brought it up, but thanks for coming with me last night. I know you don't like the dark."

"Yeah, but I don't want to ever go again to that place at night," I informed her, but I could see that she had other plans.

Suria nodded toward the teacher who entered the room. "Well, I'm going to go back there because I know that there was a reason that it's there," she finally whispered.

"It's not a ghost," I said, but I wasn't even sure; something in my head told me it wasn't.

She looked away from me to gaze at the other students in the class and then glanced back at me.

"Why do you say that?" she asked, but I didn't answer because William entered the room.

"We have a new student, and he is very good looking," I whispered, trying to change the topic. At first she didn't seem too keen to switch tracks, but then she looked to see who the new kid was.

"Is that him?" she asked. I followed her eyes to the doorway, and we watched him as he proceeded to look for an empty desk—and chose one only two seats away from me. I looked back down at the pencil I twirled in my hand and tried to focus my mind on other things.

The rest of the day went by slowly; I noticed William was only in three of my classes out of five. I ran my fingers along the cold walls while I walked from class to class.

It was my last class of the day, and I tried to focus my mind on other things. My eyes darted around the room, looking intently at the same walls I did every day. I found a calendar and stared at it for a while: the date was September 23. The bell rang and class had finally ended.

I walked to my small white 1996 Toyota. The summer air had turned humid, school had just started up again a couple weeks ago, and summer was only a faded memory. I started to unlock my car, but it was already unlocked. Weird, I thought. I looked into my car window and saw Suria sitting in my passenger seat. She waved at me and smiled as big as she could.

"Hey," I said as I sat down and started the car.

"Something weird happened today," she began to say.

"Like?" I asked.

"I was sitting in class and looked out the window, and the mist stood in the bushes. I couldn't entirely see its body, but I saw its green eyes. But the weirder part of my story was that Jane looked out the window and didn't see it. Do you think it allows just us to see it?" She paused. "I heard the humming again and instantly wanted to follow the wolf. Is that bad of me to want to follow it?"

"Who knows? I mean, it's probably not a good thing. What if it's using the humming as a lure?"

"I just want to find out what it wants, like we had been called to do this," she said as she looked out the window for it.

"I think you're getting ahead of yourself a bit. It's the day after, and you've come up with this conclusion." We soon approached her house. "Do you think we will see it at the Hot Water Dumpings today?" I looked at her, but she just shrugged.

I parked the car in her driveway, and she jumped out. I waited patiently for her. I looked toward the field by her house, and faintly in the distance shone two small green lights, the same eyes we had seen last night. They were just staring at me, and they seemed to have no body—just eyes.

"Hurry!" I yelled out the window. I searched the field where the eyes were, but now they were gone. Nervously I looked around expecting to see it closer to the car. I was a coward, unlike Suria who searched for excitement. I began to bite my nails and watched as she walked toward the car. I just couldn't imagine why people would want to search for excitement. I would much rather stay away from those things. What if the wolf wanted to hurt people at the hot springs? I pushed this thought into the back of my head.

Gracefully Suria got into the car, moving all the books and papers out of the way; her blonde hair kept falling into her face. "You saw it, didn't you?" she asked me, and I gave a slight nod.

"How did you know?"

"The humming. And the look on your face."

"Oh," I murmured.

She laughed. "You always look like you're scared of something!"

I stayed silent for a moment. I never liked it when people called me scared, but maybe it was true. It was just not a good label to have for someone my age. "Ha," I said sarcastically and smiled at her.

Luckily Ellsberg had no cops, so I drove to the Blue faster than I should have. Suria kept her eye out for the wolf. I kept my eyes straight on the road because I didn't want to see the creature at all. We ended up parking in the same spot as last night. I didn't really want to go to the Blue now because I knew the mist was somewhere nearby, but when I took a good look around and saw all the other cars alongside mine, a feeling of relief washed over me. Perhaps with all the people here, nothing would happen. I took my first step out of the car, and a slow, eerie feeling came over me that something was watching us, and I saw Suria tense up too. I stared at her, and she took a good look around before we headed on to the trail to the Blue.

"Felt it?" I asked her, just to make sure, but she didn't say anything. We ran through the trail until we could hear teenage voices. Our sandals echoed as we stepped on the last bit of twigs on the dirt trail to the Blue.

I wanted to figure things out. I was always taught that everything happens for a reason, so there must be a reason it was here. First of all, how could a mist, or whatever it was, be in the shape of a wolf, and what was the humming that was heard? It just didn't make sense.

My friend, John, ran up to greet me and yelled, "Hey! Follow me; let's get some meat on those bones of yours." He led me away from the entrance. I laughed at his odd compliment as we reached the picnic table. My hand instantly reached for a cookie, and I sat down at the table. The air was cold and the creek was steaming with heat that it had all of a sudden gained. There were three others who sat with me at the table, a couple and John, who seemed to eye the steaming creek with interest. The couple looked at me and nodded politely.

"The cookies are good, eh?" the girl said to me. I gave her a smile and nodded back; her boyfriend also seemed like he wanted to go into the creek. I watched as John poured himself more punch and ran back to the entrance to greet more people who had just arrived. I knew that within seconds they would be led to the food.

I looked over my shoulder, wanting to chat with Suria, but she was gone. My eyes scanned the area again, but it still looked the same, and no sign of Suria. A mist among the forest caught my attention; at first thought it was steam from the water, but then I looked again. It crept in between the trees, lurking in and around the bushes, and then it started to run again. I spun myself around so I could keep track and not lose where it was going, but as I spun around the last time, I wasn't facing the open field and the trees like I had expected; there was a body in the way—it was William.

"Whoa," I muttered under my breath, and I could soon feel my face grow red when I realized that I must have looked pretty stupid spinning around and around. I looked away from him.

"Looking for something?" he asked, smiling. He was only inches from me, and I felt instant relief that I had not bumped into him while I turned around.

"More like keeping track of something," I replied, and then I realized that what I had just said probably sounded odd. I was never good at first impressions, and in a way I had no interest in speaking with Will, so I stared at the grass. His hand moved out as if to shake mine. I shook his hand and looked up. I could feel my hands grow sweaty and prayed he wouldn't notice.

"I'm William."

"Hello, William, my name is Marissa." I introduced myself. I slowly turned my head so I could see if the wolf was behind him. Will must have noticed because he moved himself out of the way. Nothing was behind him except the trees and people, but I could feel the wolf's presence.

"Call me Will. William makes me sound like an old grandfather or something." He grinned as he sat beside me. He had perfectly straight teeth—I assumed from braces—and he had beautiful, passionate eyes.

"William!" Josh yelled from across the field, and I saw that Britney stood next to him, giggling like always. Will stood up, gave me another smile along with a nod, and then walked off. Just behind Josh was Suria; she stood deep in the bushes and was looking in and around the trees as if she had lost something. She tilted her head every now and then to peer around the trees, and then she would move farther in.

I walked up to her and looked into the forest with her. I didn't want to go over the bridge or even any closer to the bushes. My body shook at the feeling I had felt the night before—the feeling that someone had held me under the water and kept me down. The current was incredibly strong last night and had carried both me and Suria quite far down the bank. I studied the trees but saw no eyes or any mist that lit up the area. Why was it that the fog seemed to follow the huge wolf? I was beginning to think that the mist was a part of it—but that was impossible. I shivered at the thought of the river; why hadn't I noticed the current before? Was it always that strong? I turned and studied the creek carefully. The water was slow paced and barely moving, and I could see the bottom very clearly. I looked away from the creek and back at the crowd that sat around the table; most people were wrapped up in towels, and others were eating the food. I looked down at some of the kids in the creek and noticed the water moved by them slowly.

Suria still hadn't noticed that I was beside her; she was too focused on something in the woods that I couldn't see. Gracefully she moved around the trees and further into the woods. My eyes scanned the forest: trees, trees, trees, grass, and more trees. I still didn't see the mist or anything out of the ordinary. I looked once more, and that was when I noticed the one section of the forest that looked a bit brighter than the rest, as if a huge spotlight shined in that area. The forest seemed to grow still and quiet, but in the back of my mind I could hear the chatter of teenagers behind me. I looked harder and deeper toward the light mist; it was creeping around the trees like snakes—and there lurking in the fog lay two steady, green eyes. They stared back at us, unblinking. I couldn't see its body from where I stood and took a few steps closer, but again it had no body.

Suria gave out a short gasp, but I felt like screaming. I barely held my breath to prevent scaring the other kids. I could hear everyone laughing and splashing in the creek. Kim swam in the hot creek water, John and Jill sat on the edge of the creek, and Annie sat at the picnic table eating the cookies. Will talked with a bunch of people that I couldn't even see, and jealousy ran through my body. But my true attention never wavered from the wolf's eyes. I opened my mouth to speak but stopped. I watched the eyes take one more look at us before turning and disappearing into the woods.

Suria turned and stared at me, her eyes big.

"Is it still watching us?" I asked. She turned her head back to the bush and then back to me, still silent. I continued, "It can't be. Should we phone the cops, tell them that a wild dog is following us? Maybe they can capture it!"

"The humming stopped," she said simply, and then she walked away.

"Is that a good or bad thing?" I asked myself out loud, reluctantly following her toward the party. "Is that all you have to say?"

"We're not going to phone the cops—are you crazy?" Her eyes narrowed at me.

"Crazy enough to be thinking straight!"

"Think about it: Do you really want to phone the cops?"

"Well ..." She gave me that look. "No," I finally said. And she was right, I really didn't want to phone the cops. In fact, I didn't want to tell anybody. I felt drawn to the creature as if it was pulling me in with an invisible force. Besides, did the others even see it? If they did, they never showed it. I hit my shin on a branch and swore. Suria kept on walking, and I had to speed up to catch up to her.

I scanned everyone's faces again, and Will's eyes found mine. My face flushed. He seemed distracted, as if he wanted to come this way but didn't. He stayed with Josh but clearly wasn't too interested in the story. Josh had his arm around Brittany, and I was about to wave to Will, but instead my hand did some sort of awkward hand-bike signal. This made me blush harder. Will laughed at my awkwardness, and I made sure not to make eye contact. I turned away to face the river; it was a lot colder now, and goose bumps spread over my skin.

I noticed Suria had walked away from me and back toward the river to join the crowd. A gust of wind blew condiments off the picnic tables. I knew that this party wouldn't be going on much longer. I wanted to join the crowd, as Suria did, but I feared the bridge now and didn't want to go near it. I continued to walk toward Kim, who now snacked at the picnic table. I took one last glance at Suria and noticed that she paid no attention to the kids around her. Her eyes were rushing from one side of the forest to the other and back again, but the other kids did not notice, too caught up in their own conversations.

"Suria!" I hollered after a moment. "Come get something to eat." She looked around anxiously. "Come on," I urged. She followed my instructions and walked to me gracefully, and an odd smile grew on her face. I smiled anxiously back at her.

"So? Did you hear the humming now?" she asked the moment she reached me. I brushed some hair out of my face, and she raised her eyebrows at me.

"Uh, no. Sorry," I replied, but I wasn't too sure why I was sorry. "That thing is huge! It'd better not attack us." In my mind, I pictured the creature jumping upon us and biting off our faces. I flinched.

"No kidding," she said as she reached for an apple that sat on a table near us.

"Why is it here? Where did it come from? How come it wasn't here before?" I asked her as we sat on the bench. "Can others see it?"

"I have no idea."

I was satisfied with this answer; it seemed reasonable. Will walked up to me and sat down. He smelled so nice, like vanilla and pine trees mixed together, which I never expected would have smelled good together. His shaggy hair moved with the wind, and I couldn't help but smile at him.

"I'm going to go get my jacket," Suria said suddenly and stood up.

"Hey, Marissa," he said as we watched Suria walk off.

"Hello, William," I teased. "Are you having fun?"

"You could say that. But I don't really know anyone, so when people talk to me, I just don't know what to do," he admitted. I watched Suria disappear into the trail heading toward the parking lot. I saw the mist in the distance; it was just a mist this time and it seemed to disappear into another line of trees.

"It's a small town. You will get to know everyone pretty quick." I took another look around and pointed to a group of people. "Except those people; I don't know those people."

"Foreigners?" he joked.

"No, maybe tourists."

"Yeah, because everyone wants to come to small-town Ellsberg, where there is nothing but a small creek and some wind," he said sarcastically.

I laughed, and I thought, *It may have a small creek and some wind, but it also has a ghost wolf that wanders the trees—but no worries, it's normal for Ellsberg, no big deal.*

"Well, who wouldn't want to see some wind?" I asked halfheartedly, but my mind went back to the wolf; did it take Suria this long to get her coat, or had she wandered off? I had a feeling I would see this white mist-wolf-thing more often.

"That's exactly the reason I moved here: I needed more wind in my life," he joked again. I gave a slight laugh and watched as Suria, Daniel, and his buddies entered the clearing.

"So you're the wind watcher?" I asked.

"Of course. I have secret powers that allow me to see the wind."

"Oh really? Can you predict the weather as well?"

William laughed in response. My gaze was still upon Suria and Daniel, who had now moved away from the crowd.

"You like him?" He gestured toward Daniel. Will's question surprised me because it was odd to ask that of someone one barely knew. I had to remind myself that he was a new kid and didn't know who was related and who wasn't.

"That, sir, would be my brother." I looked at him, and he blushed.

Daniel and Suria approached us. "Hey, I'm Daniel."

"Will." They shook hands.

Suria also held out her hand. "Suria."

"I still have the same name as before," William said, and they shared a smile. Daniel looked at Will, and I could see that he wished nothing would happen between these two. I gave him a smile, and Daniel made a face at me as a joke. I heard a girl scream from the water, and instantly we all turned around to see what the commotion was. A girl ran out of the bank—the same bank I had crawled from last night—screaming about something. We all got up from the table and ran to the now crowded area.

When I approached the bank, I noticed that one of Daniel's friends—I think his name was Jake—held a green and yellow snake.

"I think that snake is poisonous!" a kid yelled.

"No it isn't!" another one yelled above the screams. Jake held the snake and laughed as he stood in the water.

"That snake *is* poisonous!" Daniel hollered, and Jake gave a little scream before throwing the snake on the other side of the bank.

"What if it poisoned me?" Jake worriedly asked as he ran out of the creek.

"Did it bite you?" someone asked.

"No."

"Then you're fine, Jake. Don't lose too much sleep over it," Daniel joked, and he started to turn away from the creek and back to the picnic table. Suria and Will followed him. I stood and watched as others dispersed and went back to what they were doing. The kids who had been in the creek seemed a bit reluctant to go back in but eventually did. Jake walked up next to me.

"Poisonous animals can't hurt you unless they bite you! I didn't even know that!" he exclaimed, "Someone else just told me that poisonous animals can paralyze their victims or put them in a coma. Oh weird!" He carried on.

"You're really excited about this, aren't you?" I asked. "You're 18, and you didn't know about poison?"

"No! Go figure! I'm sure that snake wasn't, though. I mean, I'd be dead by now, wouldn't I?"

"Maybe, or it could have chosen to bite you whenever it felt like it."

"It can choose that kind of stuff?" He seemed so excited, like a boy who had just opened his Christmas presents. I gave him a nod and walked back to the picnic table.

"They get excited about everything," I heard Will say as I sat back down next to him.

"Yeah, everything," Daniel said. Suria looked at me, and we shared a secret message about the wolf; compared to the snake, the mist was much more threatening. "Looks like everyone is leaving now," Daniel pointed out.

"Need a ride?" Will offered to me.

"I brought my car. Thanks anyway."

I stood up and grabbed one more cookie for the road. I heard Will and Daniel talking about poisonous animals and which were the most dangerous. The sky was getting a bit dark now, a dark blue with red and orange colors, and I knew that very soon night would be among us. Everyone slowly made their way to the parking lot. Some of the crowd got dressed and watched the sun set, and I could hear others drive away. I looked back up at the sky, which had now changed form and held dark black clouds that would eventually make their way to us.

"Let's head home, Suria," I said, and I walked by them to my car.

"I'm young at heart!" Daniel yelled randomly back at me, and he drove away at a miraculous speed. Suria walked over to my car, and I could see that she had no intention of leaving soon.

"You have my poor brother on a leash," I said to her as I started the car. She didn't comment, but I saw a sly smirk cross her face as she stared at me.

"You know I want to stay and see the wolf again," she said. "Let's stay a little longer, please?"

"I want to go home." I paused. "I have had enough of this mist."

"But I'm drawn to it," she admitted.

"You're drawn to any excitement, so this doesn't really count."

"You can go home," she said mischievously. "I'll stay."

I sighed and gave in. "I'm not leaving you alone, so I guess I'll stay a little longer."

"I knew you would."

I looked past her outside her window. There was a patch of forest that was lighter than the rest, and I automatically knew what it was. This was getting scary. I didn't want to stay longer at all. She nodded her head. The last bit of teenagers left the Beautiful Blue, giving us a wave good-bye.

"Fine," I grunted. The sky grew darker, and the light in the forest started to stand out more and more. The green eyes were easily seen from the car, watching us from the dark bush. We watched back, waiting for some sort of movement. What if it was planning something? Blood ran fast through my body, and I was eager to find out what would happen.

"It's dark enough," Suria said, and she stepped away from the car.

I finally answered. "Well we will just see what happens tonight." The grass shined underneath the wolf, making everything around it stand out more than usual. "Maybe we will come up with some explanation," I told her. I'd heard many times about what a ghost looked like, but it did not fit the description. I moved myself next to Suria, close enough to hear her breathing. She crouched down on the ground, and I followed her movement.

My feet scraped the gravel as I made my way to the grassy area. I carefully placed myself next to her.

"Wow," I heard Suria faintly say.

"What's wow?" I asked, but she didn't answer.

The creature was now only 10 feet away, on Suria's side of the car. The wind started to whistle in the trees. Then the feeling came back—the feeling that someone was watching. If the wolf had brought the feeling, I would have gotten it right away. The atmosphere changed once again, and my body grew sore from crouching. I became uncomfortable and stood up and the feeling grew stronger.

"It was beautiful, so sweet sounding. I must have heard it before. I really wish you could hear what it sounds like." Her brown eyes lit up. "It wants to tell us something, it wants to!"

I followed her gaze and stared at the wolf, and slowly and very carefully it made its way closer to us. My eyes met up with the mist again. The wolf stared at me, and in its eyes was a tinge of sadness. The wolf was large, very large; maybe it could be compared to a bear. My body started to shake as the mist faded away, and within a few seconds it was gone.

"I don't think it wants to tell us anything," I told her. "I think it wants to eat us for dinner."

I didn't know why she believed it wanted to tell us something. It was just music; it could be some kind of trap, like when a spider would catch a fly in its web. The web was the music, and soon we would be drawn in and trapped by the music because we followed it. This could be what the wolf wanted; it could be just waiting for the right moment. *This is horrible*, I thought. *Can it even hurt us? If it runs toward us, will we feel it?* We waited a few more moments, and then Suria stood and we headed toward the car.

"Seriously Suria, what if this is something we should be terrified of?" I said as we sat down and I started driving home.

"But we are not scared of it," she whispered.

"That's what you think," I snapped.

"But you're scared of everything," she repeated. "I don't know if you are going to join me, but I'm going to the library tomorrow." We were slient until I pulled up to her house.

"I don't have humming to calm me down," I muttered softly, and then I said louder, "We are in this together." I smiled and knew that this was why we were friends. As much as I hated this thing, I was also curious about it. I wasn't going to admit it to Suria, but I was also drawn to it.

"Yeah, we will discuss this tomorrow. Good-bye!" Maybe going to the library would be a good idea; we already had a history project that was worth working on. I liked where this was going.

I crawled into bed that night, full of questions. Everything played through my head—my conversations with Will, the encounter with the wolf, the talk with Suria, and what we would find out at the library. I fell asleep in a world of my own.

Chapter 4

As I drove to Suria's house the following morning, the sky was barely light, and the morning birds weren't even up. I knew that I was on time, but Suria wasn't outside waiting for me. I parked and waited for a few minutes, but still nothing.

Finally she came running outside and hopped in. "Sorry, I overslept."

"It's okay," I replied, and we drove the rest of the way to school in silence.

I was rather happy to have Mr. Robituson for my first class, but today things seemed to go by slowly. I tried not to look at Will, who still sat across the room.

I managed to drag myself through the rest of the classes. There was only one class left, and this made me very happy. I walked through the halls and ran my fingers along the walls. I headed into my class and sat down at my usual desk.

Suria wasn't in this class, so I had no one left to talk to, and instantly my mood lowered. It always felt that the last class went by the slowest, and I stared around the room to avoid actually having to work. John had his head on the desk, and Annie rested her head in her hand. They looked extremely bored. I didn't think science was too bad, but everyone had their own opinions. I looked out the window to see an old, rugged man look back at me, and then he carried on his walk. I thought it odd that he would look up right when I looked out the window.

I turned my head away to scan the kids again, and my vision was blocked by Will. He smiled and sat down in the empty seat on my right. "You always seem to come out of nowhere," I told him.

"Yeah, I'm like the wind. I was actually at the back of the class by myself, and then I saw this open seat." He shrugged. "So here I am."

"The person sitting to your right is your partner for this project," the teacher told the class, and he pointed at a kid. "Dylan, can you hand these papers to everyone?" I watched as Dylan got up miserably from his chair and walked toward the teacher.

"I guess we're partners," I said to William. I smiled inside, happy he'd decided to sit there. He gave me a big grin and shifted his weight toward me to see what our project was. He dark eyes glared up at me, and I turned to hide my blushing face. The class started to go by faster, and before I could even look at the clock, the bell had rung. I started to gather my stuff but felt a cold hand grab my elbow and stop me from leaving.

"Let's finish the project today," he suggested, taking his hand away quickly.

"Yeah, that sounds like a great idea." I took out a piece of paper and wrote on it. "Here's my address."

"Does seven work for you?"

"Sounds perfect."

I took another glance out the window to see that it had started to rain. The old man had disappeared from my view.

School ended and I ran to my car, trying to dodge the rain, which fell harder now. The clouds were grey with a tinge of blue, and in the distance I saw a faint rainbow. Why was it always raining? It had never rained this much. I looked inside my car and saw that there was no Suria today. Maybe she had stolen a ride from Daniel or someone else. I decided that I would go home first and drop off the books and binders that I wouldn't need.

There was a note taped to the steering wheel.

> Meet you at library at five. I stole a ride with John and Kim.
>
> Suria

Well, that made more sense. I started off for my house. As I pulled into the driveway, I saw Daniel's red Jeep across the house in a field. He had some weird parking habits. I remember when he first got his Jeep; he wanted to rip the doors off so we could just jump in his car like a superhero and drive off. It didn't happen, though, but my dad promised that this summer he would be able to finally take the doors off because Daniel proved that he could actually take care of his vehicle. I was honestly surprised he had gotten such good marks in school.

I entered the doorway and greeted my mom, and she only gave me a small wave. "Hello?" I heard her say into the phone. "No, I'm still here." Her head peeked from the kitchen. She was always on the phone, and I had no idea how she could talk to people for hours on end and never get bored. Usually if I was on the phone, the first three seconds would be okay, and then it would just get awkward.

I decided I would check and see what Daniel was doing. I walked past the TV room, expecting to see him there, but then headed toward his room. I knocked on his door.

"Yes?"

"What are you doing?" I asked as I opened the door.

"I'm heading to Jake's house. Ever since he captured a snake at the creek, he has been searching for different kinds of poisonous animals, and he wants me to come check it out." He grabbed his coat and ran past me.

I walked to my room and decided to head to the library to meet Suria.

Chapter 5

The steps to the library were very large and white. On either side of the steps were two large statues of people on horses, and right beside the statues were small benches that would usually be crowded by pigeons, but today the rain had chased them away.

I walked through the large doors and immediately spotted Suria. She looked up from the table where she sat, gave a small wave, and lifted from her chair a bit. I made my way over to her.

"Hello," she said with a smile. "If you're wondering, I have found absolutely nothing on the wolf. But I have finished our project; I came here earlier to get out of cleaning. Relatives are coming tonight."

"Thanks, that means a lot. Sorry I didn't help." I quietly took a seat as the librarian stared us down over her glasses. Piles and piles of large books were spread out all over our table, and I could see that Suria had been working hard. She picked up another large book and began to read it; there were so many books that I had no idea where to start. I picked up a book, put it down again, and began to search the library for something more interesting.

I watched as a mom gave her two small children some coloring books and picture books. At another table were two old people who looked at a large book together. I turned my attention to watch some random person because it seemed as though some confusion had grown at the librarian's table because of a book that was very overdue. I glanced at a large table that was full of jocks who weren't studying. Why were they even there?

I felt a soft tap on my arm. I turned to see Suria trying to get my attention. "Look," she said, motioning with her eyes. I couldn't see where she was looking. She leaned closer to me. "You see that really old, creepy guy standing in the corner?" I looked up and saw him. How had I missed him as I scanned the area? The way he just stood there was creepy and suspicious. He had the same stance and posture as the man outside the school.

He seemed to have noticed us staring at him. I looked away quickly and stared down at the wooden desk. Suria looked in another direction as if she was staring there the whole time. I tried to see him from the corner of my eye. Was he still looking?

"Who is he?" I asked without making eye contact. I started drawing circles in the dust layer that had formed on the surface. I wanted to look busy. Dust floated up in the air, and I couldn't help but cough.

"He is the guy who told me about the Big Blue at night. He led us to the mist creature," Suria said, stealing a glance at him, and I looked as well. He looked like he was at least two million years old.

"You think he led us on purpose?" I glanced up at her, a few strands of my hair falling into my face.

"He seemed pretty sure of what he was talking about."

"That's rather strange." A shiver crept up my spine.

"Oh my gosh! I have to go home; it's almost six. Time sure flies by." She jumped up and grabbed her books, and then she looked back down at me "My mom wants everything to be perfect and clean before they arrive." Her chair made a terrible sound as she dragged it across the floor to get up.

"I'll stay here and try to find out more stuff." I don't think she heard me because she'd already ran out the door. I studied the man again. He sported a little white beard and white hair. He had a small and faint hunch to his back, and his clothes look old, almost ancient; they were rugged with faded colors. I tried to see what book he was reading, but the title was covered in dust. An old book, I guessed. He looked at me, and I quickly looked away.

Later on I searched for the old man again, but I couldn't find him among the tall library shelves.

"None of these books say anything about a mist creature," I mumbled softy and put my head on the table, which felt cold and uncomfortable. An old, croaky voice startled me. My head flew up, and I now stared face-to-face with the old man, who sat in the chair next to me.

"Mist creature, did you say?" he asked me shyly. He had heard me?

"Yeah, I did," I replied carefully and cocked my head to the side, as if to test him. I studied his face and every detail; he was an old man, very old indeed. He looked very fragile to me. I wouldn't dare touch him, afraid he would break. He spoke again.

"Yes, long years ago there was a young lady who had written a poem about what you have just spoken. It may fit the descriptions, better than any of these books." He took a deep breath and continued. "Laura Henderson was her name, and I have it engraved in my mind, no?" I wasn't too sure if that was a question, but he carried on speaking. "Oh, it was a tragedy; no good came of it. As kind as she was, she could not escape fate." I just nodded to show I understood, even though I wasn't entirely sure.

"A young girl like you certainly doesn't want to speak with a man such as I, no? I know no such thing," he said oddly. "I shall head home now. Good day, miss."

He disappeared through the doors. The name sounded beautiful: Laura Henderson. I didn't even get a chance to comment. I took out a few more books and searched them for the poem. I looked at the books that Suria had laid on the counter and realized that none held a poem. I stood from my chair, trying to make as little noise as possible. I walked to the poetry section and began to search for the poem.

I grabbed some random poetry books from the shelf and turned the pages. No Laura Henderson. I grabbed another book and quickly flipped the pages, but no luck. Thoughts ran through my head; I couldn't understand what had just happened and how this was going to turn out. I didn't even want to have Will over for the night; I wanted to search for Laura Henderson and find out how she fit in all of this—or if she fit at all. It was all too much to take in at once, and it seemed completely insane how caught up I seemed to be getting with this wolf. Why did he have to appear out of thin air? Why was he not just a normal wolf? Why did this have to happen to me? Why couldn't some other girl see some ghost and have it on her mind all the time, instead of me? I wanted to go back to thinking about school and normal things.

I realized I stood where the old man had been. I noticed a black leather book sitting on the top of the shelf. Was this the book the old man had been reading? I picked it up and could feel the leather underneath my fingers. I wanted to talk to the old man some more. Had he known that I would go looking for the poem? Had he left it on purpose? This old man knew something, and I searched the library again to try and find him. I should have asked him his name at least.

I looked down again at the book and realized it was not a library book. Quickly I looked around to make sure no one saw me and then sneaked it into my brown jacket pocket. "Thanks again," I muttered under my breath as I walked out the door. I could feel the book bumping up against my hip as I walked, and when I reached the street I took a good look around me. The rain had stopped, and tiny puddles lay all over the library steps.

I took it out of my pocket and opened it gently with my hands, hoping it wouldn't fall apart, and then I realized that opening an old book where it could rain was not a good idea. I headed home.

My parents were serving dinner just as I arrived. I stuffed down the mashed potatoes and peas, washing it down with milk. Will would be arriving soon, and I didn't want him coming here while we were eating—that would be embarrassing. There was a knock at the door, and I told my parents I'd answer it.

"Hello," I greeted him.

"Hey, how's it going?" Will said with a smile.

"I'm fine, thank you. Want to come in?" He gave a nod and slipped into the room, following me as I made my way down the steps and into my room. I flipped the grey screen of my laptop open and saw that Will leaned over to see what I was doing. He handed me the paper that had our assignment on it.

"This project is completely stupid," he said, and my heart flipped when he smiled again. "I mean, we learned all this stuff since grade six. Anyway, I had some free time after school, so I finished most of it, but I need your opinion on a few things." He showed his work, and I looked at the paper and then took it out of his hands to study what he had done.

"Wow, that's awesome," I replied shyly. "Thanks so much." He sat right next me, and I could hear his steady breathing. I looked out my window, and for some reason I expected to see the bright green eyes outside, but there was nothing. I tensed up when I felt the feeling return that I was being watched; it was very slight, and I wasn't even sure if I was making it up and just becoming paranoid. I shifted my body away from the closed window in the hope that it would make the watching feeling go away.

I turned my attention back to the homework. "You did almost all of it; there is really nothing left for me to do. I'm sorry I hadn't contributed as much as I should have." I instantly felt guilty yet relieved that he still decided to come over.

"No, don't be. I was the one who decided to do it. It even has some glitter on it—see there in the corner?" he joked. I looked at him but then glanced back out the dark, small window. I just felt that there was something out there. It was odd, and I had never felt it before in my room.

"Why did you move here?" I asked after a few moments of silence, hoping it would distract my mind. He got up and studied the things on my shelves. The snow globes were completely eye level with Will, and he inspected all 13 of them. He turned, sat back down next to me, and looked at me. His face was only inches from mine.

"My dad grew up here and wanted to raise his children here, so we waited until the right time to move back." He stared ahead as he spoke. The watching feeling began to subside.

"What does your mom think of the move?" I asked.

His eyes moved to the floor, and his hands fumbled with each other before he looked back up to me. "She died when I was four."

"Oh, I'm sorry," I said quietly.

He looked toward me and gave me a slight smile. I wanted to take a picture of him, but I didn't have a camera, and taking a picture would be a bit creepy. His green eyes blared straight into mine, and his hair seemed to be standing in all directions.

"Hey, don't worry about it," he said. "Losing someone happens, and sometimes it just makes you stronger."

"Any siblings?" I asked, and when he shook his head I continued to talk. "Suria is an only child too; she was adopted five years ago." I tried to relate some sort of the story to him because nothing like that had ever happened to me. I hoped he wouldn't think that I was trying to set them up—mostly because I thought he was absolutely gorgeous.

"Really? Well isn't that something? Seems like everyone in this town has some sort of sweet background."

"Not me," I said, but the nightmare that had haunted me for years now crept slowly into my head. I knew not to tell Will about it, though. "Born and raised here with my brother and both parents. Ordinary story, nothing special."

"It's a good story to me; then again, any story is a good story if it's more than 10 words," he replied.

"I don't believe that," I told him.

"Prove it."

"There was a man who entered a local papers pun contest. He sent in 10 different puns hoping at least one of the puns would win. But unfortunately no pun in 10 did." I smiled proudly.

"Did you just come up with that in your head?"

"Yeah, pretty awful story, eh?"

"I would write a story on those words. Besides … there is always more to somebody than what meets the eye." His voice was strong, and yet I could detect humour.

"That's so true," I said slowly. We stared at each other for a moment, and Will shifted his body slightly and brushed the hair out of his face.

"Are the winters cold here?" he asked randomly.

"We get a bit of snow, but it's always dark in the winter. There is rarely any sun." I tensed up from the thought of less daylight; this meant more of the wolf and more darkness, and I couldn't handle darkness very well. "It'll start to get cold very soon."

His eyes shifted down at a large silver watch. "Well, I'd better go now; my dad wanted me home around this time." His weight shifted as he got off the bed. I waited until he was completely out of the way before I raised myself up.

"I'll walk you to the door," I said as I dropped my binders on the floor; they looked out of place on the lime green tiles.

I followed Will upstairs to the door, and when I looked up at him I noticed that he was almost a foot taller than me. He opened the door and took a step out, and the humid air greeted my face as I stood at my wooden doorway.

Will held his brown leather jacket draped over his arm. "I'd really like to hang out with you tomorrow," he said as he turned his head to face me.

"Me too." I beamed at him, and I saw his face flush red as he walked to his black truck and vanished. I bit my bottom lip, his words replaying in my head.

I looked around outside. I had a feeling somebody or something was watching me, but I didn't see anything but an empty street and light posts. I began to wonder if I really was growing more paranoid than usual. I walked back to my room and passed by Daniel's room.

"You like him, you like him, you like him," I heard Daniel chant as I walked by.

"Oh shut up!" I snapped. I wasn't really mad at him, though, because I didn't care if he knew who I liked. I entered my room and crawled into bed with a grin on my face; it was as if we hit it off the second we met. I couldn't wait until tomorrow.

"This might be fun," I heard Daniel say as he entered my room. He held a sandwich in his hand and took a large bite. I got up from my bed and stared at him. "Hey, I'm just saying, the reason I live is to make fun of you. I am just doing my duty—don't blame me, blame the gods." He winked and carried on eating. I shot him a weird look, and he gave me another wink before he left the room.

It wasn't until I had laid back down on my bed that I had remembered that I had forgotten to look up Laura Henderson. My eyes stared at the dark ceiling; it felt like I wasn't even blinking anymore. I guess I did have all day tomorrow to look her up. My stomach did soft flips up and down, and soon it began to move side to side. I couldn't even sleep with the thoughts of Will, Laura, the book, and the mist wolf. I just wanted time to fly by so I could see what was going to happen.

I thought about the day in my head, especially the way Will had greeted me at the door, and the way he'd reacted to what I'd said. Tiredness started to overtake my body, and I soon grew limp and dozed off to sleep.

Chapter 6

The next few days went by quickly, and one day I sat peacefully by the fire in the upstairs living room. September had just ended, and the days grew darker and chillier each passing day. I heard a large thump at the door, and I looked up from my book and waited for a few seconds; all was silent. Daniel entered the living room and seemed to be confused, because he looked at me and then behind him. We stared at each other for a few seconds without speaking a word.

"What's wrong?" I finally asked, breaking the silence. He looked at me weirdly, and we heard another large bang at the front door.

"Dude, is Mom or Dad here?" he asked.

"No," I murmured and then turned back to my book; another large bang broke the silence. That's when I realized that there really was something outside.

"Is that them at the door?" Daniel asked me. I shrugged, and he walked down the hallway and out of my sight. I paused and waited to hear my parents' voices. Daniel opened the door, and I heard the sound of heavy rain. Then there was a scream. I jumped up from the couch and ran to the door, staring at Daniel's back.

"Daniel!" I yelled. He turned around, and I saw him step away from the door. At the doorway stood Suria, who was drenched from the rain. Her hair hung straight down and dripped onto her orange sweater, and her eyes were dark—from crying or the rain, I wasn't sure. She looked at me mortified and then ran up and hugged me tightly. I hugged her back but looked up at Daniel, who shrugged, and his eyes were just as wide as his gaping mouth.

"What happened?" I finally asked, completely stunned while she cried a little on my shoulder. She looked up at me and then walked into the living room. I helped her onto the couch and sat next to her. Suria looked down at the ground, and I looked up to see Daniel staring at us before deciding to leave us alone.

Suria finally looked at me and said, "What I am about to tell you, please don't think it's weird." She seemed ashamed, but I just nodded to encourage her. "Okay, so I was walking to the store, which is only a few blocks from my house. It was still light out, and I knew that nothing would happen to me." She paused and took in a deep breath. "When I left the store, it was getting fairly dark, but I had to walk home because my parents were at my dad's office party. So when I started to walk back I saw the wolf's eyes, but its eyes showed fear and anger. ... Is that weird to say? That I saw its emotions through just its eyes? The sound coming from the wolf was so urgent and insane that I could hardly recognize it as humming." She stopped and seemed hesitant about what she was going to say next. I leaned forward as if to encourage her to keep talking. Suria stared down at the floor.

"What happened then?" I prompted.

"The eyes disappeared, and since I see them every single place I go, I wasn't too alarmed." She paused and thought about what she had just said. "I mean, it's not like I'm becoming used to seeing them, and it's not just another bird in the tree. I still get surprised and scared, but like I said before, the humming calms me."

"You see them everywhere? What do you mean?" My voice squeaked.

"Well ..." She zipped her coat up more. "For instance, the wolf would be on one side of the street and then on the other side. It seemed to move with incredible speed, but then again, air can move quickly."

"Do you think there is more than one wolf?" I glanced around the room for anything that would be out of place.

"No, I doubt it."

"Oh. Well anyway, carry on with the story."

"Sorry, it's weird to think about it now. Am I talking too much?" she asked.

"No, I want to hear what happened." I felt something begin to stir inside; I was truthfully scared to hear the rest of the story because she was still shaking.

"The eyes disappeared, and then it started to rain, and within seconds it began to rain harder. So then a person started to walk behind me. It was a dark figure, and I couldn't see any details, like the features were just black.

He started to gain on me, and even though it got closer, I still could not see his features. And then I started to run because this was just too weird for me." She paused before admitting, "He ran after me."

"You're kidding! Please, please tell me you're kidding," I said, but she just shook her head and looked down. "Then what?" I asked.

"He started to catch up to me to the point where I could hear him behind me. I started to become hysterical and knew that your house was closer, and I didn't want to go alone to my house. On my way here, I saw the mist just meters from me, and it moved as well. That's when I showed up at your house, just moments ago." She looked at me and then toward the front door. I got up and peeked around the corner, almost expecting to see someone standing there, but there was no one.

I looked back at Suria and shook my head. "You can stay here for the night, if you want."

"No, I'm going to call my parents; they don't believe in weekday sleepovers. Thanks anyway." She looked up at me. "Has anything weird happened to you?"

"No, nothing like that."

"Whenever I'm alone it seems worse, but maybe it's because I'm alone. I just feel really safe with you," she admitted.

"Safe with me?" I asked dumbly. I didn't even feel safe with myself, but someone else could? The mind was a strange place; certain people in certain situations could feel safe with a two-year-old.

I decided to tell her about Laura Henderson and how the old guy left me an ancient book that had a poem that sounded like the wolf (She was waiting to read with her friend.). I explained that I thought he'd left the book on purpose and that there was a reason I'd found it. Her large eyes watched me as I explained more about what I had been thinking. I felt uncomfortable because things like this never happened to "normal" people.

"I'll look up Laura tonight," I promised her as I finished my story.

She gave me a slight smile and looked away. "I want to go home now."

"Want a ride?"

"No, I already texted my mom to come and get me."

"Are you sure you can't stay the night? I know you're not over this; you're still shaking."

"Please, I'm okay. Just a bit shaken up, but I could have just been paranoid." I gave her a look to show her I didn't believe her, but I said nothing. I watched as she got into her parents' car before I closed the front door.

Things were beginning to get weird, and I had no idea what to expect next. I knew that I had to go look up Laura, but I was too scared to see what I would find.

Chapter 7

For the next few days we didn't speak about the mystery or even about the incident; we seemed to try to ignore it subconsciously, but I could tell that it was always on our minds. Suria got better and the wolf stopped appearing for a few days, but I was expecting to see it return. I actually tried to distance myself from Suria without her noticing, so I spent those days with Will.

Daniel and I sat on the couch waiting for Suria and Will to show up. I glanced over at Daniel, who played with some video game. Every few seconds he would give a short grunt or laugh. I heard the doorbell ring and went to the door.

"If I wasn't fighting crime in my game, I would fight you," Daniel jokingly said.

"I know, I know." I opened the door.

"Hey, guys." Suria gave me a smile and a hug and then walked around me into the house.

"Hey!" Will said excitedly and followed Suria. I wanted to tell Will about the wolf, but I felt that it was too soon; even though we spent time together, it was still something that I could only share with Suria. Besides, what would he think?

We spent the next few hours just watching a movie; Will sat next to me, Suria sat on the big recliner by herself, and Daniel laid on another couch. Will looked over at me and smiled, and he grabbed my hand. I felt my face blushing, and small butterflies grew in my stomach. I gave him a smile and squeezed his hand.

The movie finished, and we shifted ourselves around the room. I looked at Will, and he stared back at me. The living room had one big window that was attached to a sliding door; there were two couches that were a maroon reddish color with a black recliner. I looked away from Will and saw Suria staring intently out the window behind me, and slowly, without trying to make it obvious, I turned around.

I stared, searching out the window for any sign of the wolf. The sky was dark, and all I could make out was the rain. I turned back to Suria, who was still staring; her eyes didn't blink, and she seemed to be looking intently at something. I turned around again but still saw nothing.

"I thought we were having a staring contest," Will finally said to me, and I could feel him turn away from me to speak with my brother. I waved my hand slightly to get Suria's attention, and she mouthed the words, "I hear the humming."

"Should we tell them?" I mouthed back, but she shook her head to show it was a bad idea.

"I'm so good with staring contests," William continued. "But I can never win against Daniel."

"Did he make funny faces?" Suria asked, breaking from her trance and trying not to show that there was something wrong. Will nodded. "I used to make faces right back at him; it worked sometimes."

Suria quickly turned to me and gave me a look, and I instantly turned and looked out the window. The sky had grown dark and cold, the days were growing shorter, and soon snow would be falling from the heavens. Halloween was less than a month away, and the school year was off and running. I continued to search the back deck for anything weird, and then I saw it—green eyes hidden among the shadows just along the porch. They glared, and not once did they blink at us. Suria was the one who faced the window and had a better view of the creature. It still didn't seem to have a body, its floating eyes lingering outside. Even though I stared straight into the green, vibrant eyes, I didn't get the feeling of being watched. Will and Daniel had now prepared themselves for another game; Suria moved swiftly to the other side of me and leaned toward me.

"What should we do?" I asked and looked out the window again. The eyes had disappeared into the night.

"It's gone." she whispered, "so nothing, but I heard the humming …" She paused. "I seem to hear it all the time nowadays." Suria looked down as if ashamed to admit it.

"Just because I don't hear the humming doesn't mean that it's not real. We'll figure something out, and maybe I will hear it soon too," I said soft enough so that the boys wouldn't hear. She gave me a nod and then turned back around to peer outside again.

"The humming is gone now too," she said and moved back to the other couch, facing the big window. I laid myself gently down on the rest of the couch, my feet on Will's lap, who was still gaming with Daniel. I saw a small smile appear on his face.

I looked out the window and saw soft raindrops streaming down, but by the look of the dark clouds I could tell that more rain was to be expected. I stared long at Will, who didn't take his eyes off the TV, and I realized that I really liked him.

I watched Will and Daniel play for a while. Then my eyes grew tired and heavy, and I tried harder and harder to not fall asleep on the couch, but I couldn't control my eyelids any longer. It felt as if a blanket that caused sudden tiredness had swept over me. I didn't want them to notice that I was falling asleep, but I could no longer concentrate on the game. My head rested on the couch pillow, and I closed my eyes for a second to rest them. *Just a rest, I thought, nothing more than a rest; I won't fall asleep.*

The pillow was very comfy under my head, and I glanced at Suria. She still sat on the couch on the other side of the room and stared at the TV. I closed my eyes and fell into a deep sleep.

Chapter 8

I dreamed of the white wolf for the second time. Suria and I were walking down toward the Beautiful Blue, and the mist wolf was watching us. He circled us from a distance but never came close. This dream was a bit different than the first: the wolf's eyes grew large as it stared at us, and through the eyes it showed its emotions. Within seconds it changed from being sad to angry to frustrated. Nothing happened other than the wolf watching us with its gleaming green eyes. It was frightening in a way because of how normal it was, and I woke with a sudden jolt.

When I woke, the feeling came back—something or someone was watching me. I looked around now. Suria and Will had left. How long had I been sleeping? I turned to the large window and saw nothing but hard rain.

The sky was dark, and I couldn't see very much. I stood and moved closer to the window. The view hadn't changed: same old grass with the hedges, same old deck that held the BBQ, same old everything. But there was something different. My eyes scanned the lawn. Still nothing.

"Mom? Dad?" I hollered. I waited, but there was no answer; they were most likely out playing bingo. Daniel was probably in his room listening to music or out with his late-night friends. I looked around the room again; everything was dark. Suria must have turned off the TV and lights when they left. I wished they had woke me up so I could have said good-bye. I stopped looking out the window and made my way over to the door. The horrible feeling that something was watching me overtook me once again.

I wanted to go outside to see if I maybe missed something while looking out the window.

The fears of the night danced in my head, and I lay my hand gently on the cold door knob, but I couldn't bring myself to open it. Ever since my nightmare many years ago, I just couldn't bring myself to open it. Even though I was in the house, I could just feel that there was something out there that either waited for me or wanted to watch me—lure me.

The dark frightened me, especially when I was alone. I turned around and went downstairs to my room, placing my feet carefully on the cold, wooden steps. I turned into my room and quickly switched on my lights. I couldn't stand being in my own room when it was dark. Two words flashed through my head: Laura Henderson. I ran and grabbed my silver laptop from my desk and gently fell onto my bed with it on my lap.

Many results showed up; I clicked on the one that appealed to me most and began to read.

Laura Henderson 1853–1888.

She had died at the age of 35. How terrible. I continued to scroll down the page and saw paragraph after paragraph of useless description. In the corner of my eye, I saw the old dusty book from the library on my shelf and decided to read the description of her later; right now I was only interested in what the poem said. How much did that old man know? Or maybe he didn't and was just lucky. It hit me now that I still didn't know his name. That was rude—he'd never introduced himself. Although I guess I hadn't either. But I was a teenager; we were supposed to wait for the adults to talk first.

He happened to mention some kind of poem that described the wolf. What was the name of the poem again? I thought back to the day in the library and realized that he hadn't said much, and the stuff he did say seemed based on another vocabulary. I got up and snatched the book, flipping through the pages, but each page in the book was blank and contained some little wrinkles or was half ripped. I flipped page by page. Every single page I had flipped through was blank; absolutely nothing was written in it. An entire book made of blank pages? Unbelievable, I thought. Was this some kind of joke? Was there even a poem in the book? But there it was, just pages from the end, in old writing and very small print.

The Guardian
By Laura Henderson
Among the stars you may find them.
They come as a mist.
Best seen in the shimmering full moon,
Each is picked out. A song comes along;
Only one may hear their music.
Crystal sparkling eyes
Always looking after you.
They are not alive but walk among the dead.
Your Hero, Your Guardian.

I sat and read the poem over and over; it did sound somewhat like what I saw. But it just didn't make sense. Was this poem just a poem she came up with in her head one day? I wished she was still alive so I could ask her what this all meant—then things could easily be over and done with. What did she know? Where was she buried? Suria heard some humming. Was that the music? Did the mist wolf seek Suria out because she was some distant relative of Laura? It seemed quite possible because Suria was adopted, and no one knew her family history. I carefully placed the book down; it seemed more precious now that I had read the poem, even if it did contain useless blank pages.

The laptop screen flashed open to the website I had left it on. My eyes scanned the small words, but none of it mentioned her and how she had died. Was she the ghost? No, that seemed too creepy. If it was, why would she be back as a wolf? Or why would she still be on Earth if she'd died? Maybe it wasn't her. My fingers clicked on another website that seemed to have more information. The poem mentioned that they walked among the dead. What does that even mean? I couldn't help but picture people rising from the grave and walking around as some crazed zombies.

Bibliography of Laura Cahier

Laura-Anna Cahier was born in 1853 on May 2 in Locktown. She was born and raised by her parents, Anna Grace and Walter Adam Cahier. Laura lived a normal life with good marks in school, but she had a passion for poetry. Even at the age of seven, Laura could write poetry better than anyone in the school. At the age of 10, she had a book published with all her favourite poems that she wrote. As the years passed, Laura found another passion: teaching. She often would volunteer in schools, hospitals, and veterinary clinics to teach and take care of needy people and animals.

At 15, Laura started taking extra courses in English and began spending all her time around animals and children. Once she graduated from school at the age of 18, she went to university in the English department to become an English teacher.

At university, Laura met Rupert Henderson (1851–1891), and they had a child, Emily-Laura Henderson, on March 2 (1879–1891). Soon after Emily was born, Laura married Rupert in 1882.

Rupert spent many long weeks working on the Railway leaving Emily in the care of Walter Adam and Anna Grace Cahier while Laura was away for work. Walter Adam Cahier worked to help Chinese immigrants with bunkers and the train work. Within a few months after the wedding, Walter and Anna were murdered; the killer was never found.

At the age of 34, Laura became deathly ill with an unknown sickness, and she passed away a year later in

1888. It was believed that the illness was caused by depression from the death of her parents, especially her father, who had been very close to Laura. Emily, who had been surprisingly close to her mother, did not take Laura's death very well. Additionally, Rupert became a heavy drinker after she passed.

Three years later her daughter and husband perished in a fire in 1891.

The unknown sickness caught my attention. One would suspect that the doctors would have been able to find some cure for her or relieve her from some pain. But I have heard of people who got depressed due to a traumatic event, and it caused their health to spiral downhill. It seemed as though she was a nice lady and had a kind heart. It would be terrible to die so young, I thought again. It was completely possible to die of a broken heart.

I soon grew more curious about her parents' deaths, and it made me sick to the stomach to think of people taking the lives of others. I also wanted to find out about the fire that had killed the rest of the family. Death was interesting to me—as long as it didn't happen to me or my family. My fingers scrolled down the screen searching for another article on either family member's death.

I wanted to tell Suria about what the article said, but it was pretty late at night. My head raced around each separate detail. If Laura was so good with animals, was that why she could possibly be the wolf mist? I wanted to know—I needed to know. It felt mandatory for me to find out. Then I found the article about the fire.

On July 22, 1881, a large fire broke out at the Henderson house. The farm was located just outside Round River. An anonymous caller informed the police that a fire was consuming the house. The mystery caller was never found. When the fire trucks and police forces arrived at the

> *house, it was too late. Rupert George Henderson's body was found in the main bedroom of the house. He suffered third-degree burns on his face and back.*
>
> *Police could not locate 10-year-old Emily Laura Henderson, who resided in the house with her parents. However, officials Found suspicious marks that led to the tree line. Further details have been withheld.*
>
> *Investigators never discovered the source of the fire. The police closed the case, and Rupert and Emily Hendersons' deaths were blamed on the fire that also destroyed the house. Ten-year-old Emily's body was never found and was presumed consumed by the fire. Rupert and Emily were laid to rest in a small graveyard located southeast of the small town of Collymed.*

Then it dawned on me: maybe the wolf was just looking for Laura. The wolf could have been her guardian or something like that, and now it was just trying to find her again. All I had to do was go to her gravestone and hope that the wolf would follow, and they could be reunited! Collymed wasn't even that far from Ellsberg, and maybe the wolf showed itself to us because we lived close to the burial site. Perhaps Suria and I were distant relatives of Laura—most likely Suria, because she could hear the strange music.

Somewhere deep inside me I felt like I needed proof that these events actually happened and that the people were real. I read the article over again. I wonder if something else happened to Emily. Where would one find the time to get the body while the house was burning to the ground? What were the strange marks on the ground? The world just seemed to get crueller and crueller as the years went by, and all we would be left with would be our horrid memories and regrets.

I looked up her name to see if the town had any recent record of Emily after the fire, or if the case was reopened. It was sad to think she died in the fire or had some other horrible death. No one could keep a girl hidden for so long. She was dead for sure now—the fire had happened in 1891, 118 years ago. What did she look like? What did the whole family look like? Maybe this would make the past more real.

My fingers scrolled down the page, where it showed three pictures of the family.

The first picture was Laura holding her small daughter. Laura was the most beautiful person I had ever seen. She had light hair that hung past her shoulders, and her smile was soft and gentle. It looked like her eyes were chocolate colour, but it was hard to tell because the picture wasn't the greatest quality. It was very old, ragged.

I scrolled down the page and took a look at the second picture. It was one of the whole family as they stood next to each other. Rupert had his arm around Laura. He sported a big beard and was bald on the top of his head. His eyes were cold and hard and very dark; his face showed no emotion. Laura had her hair tied in a bun, and she had a big smile on her face. She held hands with Emily, who looked to be four or five. Emily's eyes were squinting due to the sun, and she was smiling ear to ear. It almost looked like the perfect family, but Rupert did not fit into the mould—he looked miserable, really.

I looked at the last photo, on the bottom of the page. It was a portrait of Emily. This photo was only a head shot of her. Her light hair was curled in almost perfect ringlets that hung loose on the top of her shoulders. Her head was tilted to the side, but instead of the smile and happiness she had in the photo before, her face looked sad and her eyes drooped. Her smile looked like it had been forced. She looked to be older in this photo. There was only one reason she looked so upset, I thought: her mom must have passed away already.

I couldn't stare at the sad woman's face anymore and quickly closed my computer and put it away. I evaluated all the information I had just consumed; it was enough for one day. Tomorrow I was going to the Metal Stone Graveyard to return the mist-wolf to Laura. He must not know where her body was, so he needed help, guidance. Would he just disappear from then on? Would he crawl into the grave with her? I didn't know how this plan was going to work, but I felt had everything solved. Tomorrow I would tell Suria. I thought about this plan over and over again in my head.

My heart started to beat faster. I finally had everything solved—I was going to finish this mystery once and for all. It would soon be at an end, and I could put it to rest and go on living my life as a normal teenager. A smile crossed my face as I hoped I wouldn't have to tell Will about any of this; I didn't know how I would tell him if it came to that point. I felt my heart beat faster at these thoughts, and soon enough I had drifted off to sleep to the rhythm of my heart.

Chapter 9

I woke up and jumped out of bed. It was going to be a good day! I couldn't wait to see Suria's face when I told her that I had everything solved. It fit so perfectly; there was no way I could be wrong. I was positive everything would be back to normal by the end of the day.

I got dressed in a hurry, and my stomach had soft butterflies in it because of the news. I drove up to her house and started to honk my horn repeatedly. I saw Suria open the white door on the side of her house. She looked over at me and gave me the "one minute" sign. I couldn't blame her, though, because I had shown up at her house almost 20 minutes earlier than usual.

I watched her run down the driveway and jump into my car.

"Suria, I got everything figured out! Like with the ghost-wolf thing!" I yelled at her. I was not making sense, but she seemed to understand.

"Really?" she asked, her face lit up. "Tell me everything!"

I told her about the conclusion I had come up with, and I recited as much of the Laura Henderson's poem as I could remember. I told her that the ghost-wolf was looking for his owner and that he must be her guardian or something. I ignored the fact that my plan wasn't entirely foolproof. I didn't even know if I was actually going to do the right thing, but I could just imagine what would happen if he found his owner. I didn't quite know how it all worked, but I had the majority of it figured out. I tried to reassure myself of everything now, driving to school slowly and trying to explain as much as I could to Suria. Her face lit up as I talked and talked.

"If we go to the graveyard, you think the wolf will just crawl into the grave?" Suria asked as we headed toward the school. "Would you even go inside a graveyard?"

"Well, someone has to show the wolf where Laura's grave is located." I hesitated for a moment and looked toward the sky. "I don't know about going in, though. I just don't know."

"This will be fun. How exciting!" she teased.

"You are joining me, right?"

"The relatives are still over." She brushed some of her long blonde hair out her face. "I'll have to see."

We parked and walked into the school. The sky was grey and cloudy, almost like it was going to rain again. I counted the posters on the walls as Suria was still absorbing the information I had just told her.

"And," I added, "I think you can hear the humming because—"

"Because I must be Laura's distant relative or something?" she cut me off; her brown eyes were wide.

"Exactly my thoughts!" I said excitedly.

"When do you want to go?"

"I was hoping tonight because the rest of the week we're expecting really bad weather." I scratched my head. "I know where the graveyard is and everything."

"Maybe," she said again.

I knew that she had family over, but I didn't want to go by myself; frankly, the idea terrified me.

"I promise, though," Suria continued, "I'll try my best to come tonight. I'll spend time with my family until seven, and then you can come over and I'll tell you whether or not I can make it tonight," she said and smiled at me. "No guarantees."

I smiled at her and continued to my classes. Will waited for me at my first class, and we exchanged a quick hug before both of us entered the class. His hair was flipped the same way as usual, but it was shorter.

The day went by more quickly than usual. I sat in my second-to-last class and attempted to draw the mist-wolf, which was a lot harder than it seemed. It was hard to draw something that was almost invisible.

"Hey, what are you drawing?" Will questioned as he leaned over toward me, getting almost right in my face.

"I'm trying to draw a wolf," I whispered back to him.

"Why are you drawing a wolf?" he asked, his face showing he was interested in what I had to say. He leaned toward me again. He flashed his teeth at me, and I felt my face grow red. *Perhaps I should tell him about the ghost wolf.* We had spent quite a bit of time together, and I silently prayed that he wouldn't think I was crazy.

I made up my mind to tell him. "Because there is ..." My mind went blank; I had no idea how I would begin to tell him.

"Yes, Marissa?"

"Do you believe in ghosts?" I blurted.

"I don't believe in ghosts; that stuff is just silly. That never happens, it's just plain silly." He laughed, not noticing that my feelings had been hurt. I looked at him, my lips pressed together.

"What were you going to say?" he asked, but I didn't say anything back to him. He quickly grabbed my hand and led me out the door to the next class. "I wanted to know if you wanted to hang out tonight with me," he continued and gave me a kiss on the forehead, something he had not done before. "I have some movies lined up for tonight!"

"I'm going to a graveyard tonight," I told him, instantly regretting what I said. I hoped he wouldn't ask my reason for going there, especially since he knew those things terrified me. He looked at me with a weird face. "It's just something Suria and I are going to do. It's just to prove something that we read about," I lied. Guilt flushed through me, and I watched his face turn into a smile.

"Which graveyard?" He leaned closer to me, and a whiff of vanilla pine floated through the air. My heart began to race.

"Collymed. It's about an hour away." I smiled innocently.

"Yeah, I know," he promptly said, with a hint of some sort of sarcasm. "I'll call you later, okay?" I gave him a slight nod as well as a kiss on the cheek. We still hadn't gone any further than holding hands, and inside I longed for a kiss. Then I remembered what he said during class. How was I supposed to tell him now about this mystery if he thought things like this were silly? The rest of the day went by slowly.

By the time I reached my car, only three cars were left in the school parking lot, but none were Will's black truck. My heart fell for two reasons: I couldn't tell him about this ghost thing now without looking stupid, and I had lied to him about something big that was happening in my life. Daniel's truck drove past me, and in his passenger seat was Suria. She gave me a big smile and waved, and Daniel honked his horn.

I watched the time closely as each hour passed by. I wanted seven to come by quickly so I could just go to the graveyard with Suria. It would have been smarter to leave right for Collymed after school, but Suria needed to spend time with her family before convincing them to let her go, and I felt that the moon would be needed in this plan. More than a month had gone by since the first spotting of the wolf, and tonight the moon would shine like a diamond in the sky. But what would happen if I was wrong? If my guess didn't come true, where would I go from there? If I had it wrong …

I could try to go find that old crazy guy right now. He knew something that I didn't—he told me about Laura Henderson. Besides, there was this vibe about him that I hadn't felt with anybody, like a cold, dead silence came from him.

I thought back to what I'd read in the articles. They gave Emily an empty grave, which was a good thing. It was really the thought that counted, right? Blood rushed from my head, and I was getting excited all over again.

I then thought back to my and Will's relationship. We'd been dating for about three weeks now, and we'd only held hands while walking down the hallways, and we cuddled in front of the TV. My mind travelled back to the first time we hung out; we just sat on the couch and chatted. His soft hands would play with mine, and butterflies fluttered in my stomach. Halloween was just around the corner, and soon November would be upon us. By then Will and I would have known each other for a while. I sat down and put on a movie to pass the time, though I didn't even pay attention. I glanced at the clock on my phone every few seconds until it finally read 6:49 p.m.

"Finally!" I muttered under my breath as I ran to my car. I drove to Suria's house and ran to her doorstep. The night was almost a clear sky, enough to see the dimmer, smaller stars. I glanced around as I drove; the streets were empty except for a few random cars. No eyes, no wolf, no feeling of being watched. It must have rained a little while I was inside because there were little puddles on the ground. I placed my feet carefully, making sure I wouldn't slip on one.

"I can't come, I'm really sorry," Suria apologized the instant she saw me at the door. Her hair was tied back into a tight pony tail, and her face was bare of makeup. She wore her red badminton shirt and long, chequered pyjama pants. "Do you want to come in for a bit, though? You can come meet my crazy grandfathers."

"Sure," I responded sadly. I didn't want to go on a one-hour drive by myself. I wasn't the greatest driver given the nighttime. "One second, Suria. I'm going to just call Will and see if he wants to join."

"You're a brilliant gal." I watched her leave before I pressed the call button.

I explained quickly on the phone to him what I wanted to do that night (most of it slightly twisted) and asked if he wanted to join me. It surprised me that he agreed with no second thoughts; it was probably because he'd wanted to hang out with me earlier. He agreed to meet me at Suria's house. I stood on the doorstep as some little kids raced by my feet and out the doorway.

I made my way into the living room and heard loud, angry talking coming from within. The room was a dark mahogany with greenish coloured furniture. I turned the corner to see four elders playing poker. *Must be the grandparents*, I thought. One man wore an old tuxedo and had no hair on the top of his head; he sat next to a very old lady who looked like she had no idea what was going on. Her eyes darted all around the area, and her white hair was slicked back into a tight bun.

The other two intently played the game. The second man had a crazy-looking hat on, and his partner had equally crazy hair. Suria came to my side, and we watched the four get mad at each other. The front door opened from behind me and shut with a large bang. The next second I felt a pair of rough hands grab my side. "Hello," Will whispered in my ear. I turned slightly to greet him with a smile. He grabbed my hand, and with his other he tucked a loose strand of my curled hair behind my ears. His hands were coarse, and I could feel every groove and scar that had been engraved over the years.

I soon got distracted because the grandparents' fight had grown louder. They weren't even arguing about the game anymore. I listened briefly before I turned my attention back toward Will. Suria was giggling silently to herself, and Will stared, mouth gaping, at the fighting foursome. They seemed to be getting mad at each other because the one in the tuxedo, Leo, thought that the sun rose because the white chariot pulled it across the sky. I instantly realized that Leo was referring to the Greek myths—he thought they were real?

"No! That is not real, Leo!" crazy-hat man yelled. His name was Maldo.

"Maldo, those chariot riders are hard at work to create day for us!" Leo sulked and crossed his arms to indicate he was going to sulk. "Let's just play poker."

Apparently these four always fought—well, three of them, at least. The one old lady still looked like she had no idea what was happening. I watched as they grew angrier and angrier with each other. The poker game had turned into a world war among the grandparents, and I soon expected eyes to be poked out.

"We'd better leave," I laughed, grabbing Will's hand and leading him toward the front door. I didn't want to get involved into the fight that the elders were having. I was surprised that they didn't even see us watching them. "Good-bye, Suria," I said sweetly. She winked and then smiled back before I closed her front door behind me. I wasn't going to admit that I was worried and terrified about this plan, and a part of me didn't want to play it through.

"Let's go in my truck," Will told me as he unlocked it. I gave him a short nod of agreement because I hadn't wanted to drive in the first place.

The sky slowly faded to a deep black, and even more stars poked out. I stared at the sky and tried to name as many constellations as I could. He opened the door for me—what a gentlemen—and then got in and started the car.

"How long is the drive again?" Will asked as he got into the car, and soon the yellow lines passed under us.

"About an hour. I've only passed Collymed a few times, to go to Suria's family's farm." I glanced over at him; he was concentrating on the road. I felt really safe with him. Will's truck had black leather seats and could fit six people in it, three in front and three in the back. I looked in the back seat and saw his red gym bag.

"Hand," I said lightly. He glanced over and grabbed my hand. "Now that's better." He nodded and continued to watch the road.

"So why must you urgently go to a graveyard tonight?" Will teased, and our eyes caught each other.

"It's a long story."

"Oh," he said quietly. "May I know why? 'Cause to be honest, it seems rather impractical to be doing this. If some weird thing is going to happen, hopefully it will be something like superpowers on my part, because that would be superb."

"I know. I'm sorry to have dragged you along." I smiled innocently at him. "But I wouldn't be able to go by myself." Why did he have to be the reasonable one? Then again, why did I always have to be the scared one? I knew it was because of the nightmare that I had at a young age—a nightmare that I would never tell anyone, not even Suria.

The drive was mostly silent for the way there, except for a few conversations. I stared out the window most of the time, counting three shooting stars. The sky was completely clear of clouds and glittered with countless stars for the first time in a long time. My main goal wasn't to look for falling stars but to see if the mist-wolf was following me. I was glad that it wasn't raining this night, or it would have made walking through the graveyard difficult. The wolf was the main reason Will and I were driving all the way to an unknown town, to an unknown graveyard for an unknown person.

I noticed a sign in the distance and leaned forward to read it. On a red, bricked sign in big bold letters read the word "Collymed."

"We're here. Do you know where the graveyard is?" Will said as he leaned forward to start reading the names of streets. His hazel eyes scanned the roads.

"It should be on Mirror Drive Road." I too started reading the names of the streets—Cornerstone Road. Lingston Street. Mirror Drive Road. "There it is!" I pointed out.

Will turned down the road. Full-sized trees lined each side of the road, which caused the street to look dark and full of shadows. We drove all the way down to the end of the street. I felt shivers down my spine when I spotted the entrance to the graveyard.

The huge gate had a metal cross on it, and over the gate was the name Metal Stone Graveyard.

Will parked the truck across the road from the graveyard entrance, and I got out slowly. The air was chilly with an odd atmosphere to it—something that had been happening a lot lately. The gate was almost four meters up and five meters wide. I hoped it wasn't locked as I walked up to it and looked in. Now I wished we had arrived sooner because the moon was the only light that shined on the gravestones. Will walked over to me and slid his hand into mine; perfect fit. The lock was worn and easy to break open. He used his other hand for us to fit through it, and he led us into the creepy surroundings of the dead.

"Come," he whispered.

"Uh …" I muttered, too scared to speak. Zombies, I thought to myself.

The gate screeched against the ground as it moved in the breeze. I noticed Will winced at the sound. Holding his hand made my phobias of the night slowly fade away, but the feeling of being watched now hovered heavily in the air, and shivers ran down my spine and to my toes.

My eyes started to scan the gravestones, which lined up perfectly in rows, each with a different shape and size. Some seemed to have castles built around the buried bodies, and others had just tiny, metal plates. It seemed like the gravestones carried on and on forever—endless rows of waiting zombies. I didn't know where to start looking for the Henderson family headstones. The graveyard didn't have much light now, and I could see that the lampposts were broken—smashed.

"We must find a certain family," I said. "The last name is Henderson, and there are three in the family." I noticed William gave me strange look, as if to tell me that I was crazy.

"What are their first names? Just in case there are more Hendersons," he said.

"Emily, Rupert and Laura."

"We should split up then. It will take longer if we stay together and look at each headstone." Half his face gleamed with moonlight. It was a good idea, but I didn't want to be alone. I should've known that it would come to this. The sooner I could leave this place, the happier I would be … even if it did involve going off by myself.

"Okay, I'll start on the south side, and you start on the north side," I said, and he let go of my hand, breaking the link between us, and handed me a small flashlight. This impressed me greatly because he always seemed to think ahead, even if he was unsure of the situation—this boy was smart and seemed to have some sense, unlike myself. We went our separate ways. I smiled at him and glanced back to see him disappear into the shadows and be swallowed by gravestones.

The ground under my feet was moist from the rain that had fallen earlier that day. Moss and vines had taken over the ground, intertwining with the grass and soil. I swore under my breath when a vine looped too far above the ground and I tripped over it.

The flashlight guided me through the graveyard as I scanned the names and dates on the gravestones. Every once in a while I would switch the flashlight off and on so that I could see if the light mist (or the eyes) was anywhere in the trees. The feeling of being watched lingered heavily around the edge of the trees. The night had grown colder with chilly gusts of wind that blew frequently. If I was a completely normal teenager, I would soon have to worry about what to dress up as for Halloween. Then I found it odd that I was worried about Halloween even though I had bigger events in my life.

There was nothing in the trees, not even the sign of the wolf, and in the back of my mind I kept wondering what Will was thinking and if he was okay. He must have thought that I had brought him here for no reason. I looked over to where he was and saw a small light in the distance from his flashlight. He had covered more gravestones than I had; the darkness had caused me to be more careful, afraid something would jump out and swallow me. Slowly I kept on walking, reading the words, and after every headstone I expected to see the familiar names of the family. I found something else.

Paula Bloom Wood
2000–2004
With a laugh that could light up the whole world
RIP

She had died at the age of four? I couldn't help but feel very sorry for that little girl. Her poor family only knew her for a short time. I wondered how she died. She missed all the great experiences of life like learning how to ride a bike for the first time, finishing her first chapter book, and growing old with the ones she loved.

"I found it! I found it!" I heard a deep voice in the distance yell. I looked toward his direction and started running toward it, avoiding all vines and gravestones that could possibly trip me. Will wasn't too far off from where I was, but I could barely make out his figure. The moon peeked out from behind the tiny clouds, the whole Earth lightened up, and now I saw Will's features.

Long, green vines had grown everywhere, weaving in and out of the ground as if it were an ocean. The graveyard stretched out forever; there must have been graves that had been here for many centuries. I was a bit nervous and tried to lighten my mood with some jokes. People were dying to get in here. Wait, I had a better one. I bet this graveyard was in the dead center of the town. I walked through many rows of stones at a quicker pace; the idea of not being alone anymore sent relief through my body.

"Where are you exactly?" I yelled.

"Over here!" he called out again. In the distance I saw a figure waving his arms frantically.

"I'm coming!" I bellowed toward him. I turned off my flashlight and continued to walk toward Will. I searched the woods for any sign of the mist; the trees were completely silent, and not even the light of the mist-wolf was to be found. How would my plan work if the mist-wolf wouldn't cooperate? Would he even show up at all? One gravestone caught my eye; it had a grey gargoyle that sat perfectly on a stone platform with wings that reached out for a meter. The face seemed to be screaming out in pain and agony with pointy teeth in every corner of its mouth. I would never want such a creature anywhere where I was—especially in my bedroom.

I reached Will and looked down at the three gravestones that lay next to each other. Each was legible in perfect script—Rupert George, Laura Anna and Emily Laura—but something else caught my attention: two other familiar names. There standing next to the Hendersons were perfectly round, intact headstones with the names Walter Adam Cahier and Anna Grace Cahier. Their graves were right next to Laura's grave. The article said that Laura was close to her father, and I couldn't help but picture all the times they would have spent together, like when he would sit her down and tell her stories of his past, or when Laura got her heart broken for the first time, and her father was there to hold her and love her. Each grave had its own summary of the person in 10 words or fewer—usually about the life he or she had led and how wonderful he or she had been. It saddened me that all these people had laughed, lived and loved. It was sad to describe an entire life in so few words, like it was just another death. I mean, it was, but it included a life.

"There they are," I whispered to myself. Each had suffered his or her own terrible death.

"Now what?" Will took a step toward me and gently put his hand on my shoulder, wrapping the other around my waist.

"Umm," I hesitated. "Just wait …"

"Marissa?" His voice was smooth.

The moon peeked out of the clouds again, brightening things up. Will stood next to me, and I saw his eyes staring at me. Those beautiful emerald eyes blazed right into mine.

"It should be here, the wolf—he should be right here," I said. Disappointment flushed through me. My plan should be working; there was no major flaw to it, just maybe some minor errors. The wolf should have followed us and crawled into Laura's grave, so where was he? The trees were empty of life and only contained darkness.

"What wolf?" Will questioned me, and a whiff of his scent fluttered through my nose. I could feel his body right against mine, so warm and comforting. I looked around the forest again in the hopes of seeing the wolf.

"It's a long story," I said. "It should be right here, though."

I continued to look around the yard, searching the edges of the woods. No sign of the wolf, or even sign a fog. I felt like crying. Will continued to stare at me, clearly noticing my disappointment. I could tell from his face that he had many questions, but he kept silent and glared at me. I felt his grip grow tighter on me, and he slowly pulled my body toward him, his fingers holding onto my side. With his hand around my waist, he began to turn me around so that I faced him now, and the moon's light was directly on his face. A smile crept across his face, and I had to look away to avoid turning red.

His right hand slid up to my face, touching my cheek. I wrapped my arms around his neck; he was the perfect height. I twisted my hands together so that he was locked in my grip, and slowly he started to lean his face toward mine with his eyes closed. I followed his lead and closed my eyes as well. I could hear his heart beat faster and assumed he could hear mine.

His lips soon touched mine. The end of the world could have happened right then, and neither of us would have noticed. The kiss lasted a few seconds, and then I began to feel him pull away from me. I looked up at him; his eyes stared at me and his cheeks flushed. He pulled me closer into his chest, and I could feel the cotton of his sweater under my cheek.

"Marissa ..." he whispered into my ear. I remained silent, too happy to speak. He spoke again. "Will you be my girlfriend?" My body stiffened, and I turned to face him. His lips were in a tight line, but I saw a smile in the corner. *Smart boy*, I thought. *A graveyard is the perfectly place to act manly for a girl afraid of the dark.*

"Yes, of course," I said to him. His face was only inches from mine now, and I couldn't help but analyze his face. Will smiled.

"We should go," he quickly suggested, and he looked down, cheeks still red. "Don't want people to get suspicious now, do we?" My face flushed also, and I started to take a step back from him and make my way back to the entrance.

Then it happened. My heel hooked onto a vine that had sprouted in front of Mr. Henderson's marble gravestone, and I felt myself fall backward. The vine had wrapped itself around the back of my foot and pulled me down. I watched as Will's hand reached out to catch me, but he was too slow. I quickly turned my body in the split second I had to react so that the gravestone would hit only my left side. I hit the gravestone and rolled off onto the moist ground.

Pain jolted throughout my entire body as the gravestone broke under my weight and shattered into different sized pieces.

Will stared at me, mouth open in shock, and he looked uncertain about what to do. I closed my eyes tight as I lay on the ground, taking in the pain and waiting for it to go down. My left hip hurt the most, and it hurt to make any movements. I could feel my body start to swell and bruise.

"Are you okay? Marissa! Open your eyes," Will yelled. I obediently followed his orders and opened my eyes. I glared up at him, and the flashlight in his hand was blinding. It took a few seconds before I could see clearly around where I had fallen.

"Help me up." I reached out for his assistance. He pulled me up so that I stood next to him.

I stared down at the small, shattered marble pieces on the ground.

"Oh no," I moaned.

"You broke Rupert's gravestone!" His voice was urgent. "We must leave—I'm pretty sure this is a criminal offence. That was supposed to be cement …" He whispered the last sentence softly. "Weak cement? A small girl broke it? She broke the gravestone, the cement gravestone. Was that even cement? Marble? Broken …" He carried on murmuring before finally noticing me again, and he snapped out of it. "Let's go, Marissa."

I remained where I was, mesmerized by what I had just done—the top corner of the gravestone had broken off, and evidence lay everywhere. A huge gust of wind blew by us and the feeling of being watched surrounded me! The moon had disappeared completely behind the clouds, which had laid a dark blanket upon the ground. Usually being under a blanket was a secure haven, but a dark blanket over the earth was too much for me—nowhere to hide. William held out his hand and I took it. It felt like the kiss was a long time ago, like it had happened many days ago, the atmosphere had changed that greatly.

"Wait." His flashlight darted back toward the ground. "Look, what is that pink thing in the ground?"

"Where?"

I quickly looked down to find myself staring at a small book that was hidden among the dirt and rubble, and I instantly reached down. With a quick tug I freed the pink book. It was encased with a glass covering, and the lock on it had broken over the years, but it had kept the book in perfect shape. I freed the book from the glass case and dropped it among the rubble of the marble tombstone, so that now all I had in my hand was the bare, fuzzy book. How had this journal gotten hidden under the headstone? Obviously somebody didn't want anyone to find it, but in a gravestone? Out of the corner of my eye I saw William glance at the entrance. The book had tiny, hand-sewed, cursive lettering on it.

"I never noticed this before," I pointed out.

"Marissa ..." Will urged again, tugging on my hand.

I stared at the book, trying to make out the small lettering. "Oh," I breathed as I opened the little lock and flipped the book open. The pages felt as if they were going to fall apart, and many edges had been worn out or ripped away; some seemed to have been torn out on purpose. I read the inscription on the inside cover.

To My Precious Little Girl, Emily Henderson.
I Will Love You Forever, My Child.
From Your Mother.

Laura

It was a diary of some sort, and I quickly flipped through the pages. The diary obviously belonged to Emily, the daughter. I cringed at the idea of her burned body being dragged on the ground and into a forest. Had she been stolen or kidnapped, or maybe someone had helped her escape the fire? Didn't the article say Laura loved to teach? The first page contained the alphabet, and some pages consisted of a very big neat *A* and then a bunch of messy, little *A*s. This system continued all the way to the letter *Z*, and then the rest was very untidy, hardly readable writing, but it seemed to be correct spelling from what I could tell. I didn't have time to read it right then because Will kept tugging at my hand.

"Okay, let's go," I said.

"Sorry to pull you away, but what if someone comes?" Will said as we started to walk.

"No, it's a good point," I said, keeping my head down so that I wouldn't see any shadows.

"Sorry," he said again. "I just see the reasonable side of things, and leaving now is the reasonable thing to do."

I tucked the diary safely away in my jacket pocket as Will's pace began to quicken, and eventually I was on the verge of running to keep up. I carefully watched the ground to make sure I wouldn't fall on another vine, often retracing Will's exact steps. By the time we reached the gate, we had to stop and catch our breath. The moon was now high in the sky and hid behind clouds, but the graveyard still contained the blanket of darkness. Will carefully opened the gate, making sure to be quiet. I turned around one last time and stared at the graveyard, and even though it was still dark, I could picture Rupert's gravestone lying in pieces on the moist ground. What would people think? Did they have grave watchers? Or was that only in the olden days? I couldn't even bring myself to picture someone who hung out in a graveyard all night, waiting for people to ring their bells for service. I had read that in the olden days, people thought that the dead were sometimes just sleeping, and they put a bell above the ground near the coffin attached to a piece of string so that if the people "woke up," they could ring it and be rescued.

"Hello? Is someone there?" A deep voice hollered in the distance. Apparently they did have sentry duty here. I quickly looked back and saw a bigger flashlight that got larger and larger; the guy who protected the graveyard was coming fast. He was north of where the entrance was, where we were. I couldn't imagine that this guy often saw much excitement, but it was a really big graveyard, and if people were buried with jewellery, I guess some sick fools would dig them up.

"Go!" Will quickly pushed me through the open metal gap and followed behind me. He looked around at the street and then turned back to the huge, metal gate and closed it.

"Hurry, to the truck." He grabbed my hand again and led me. "People may think we were trying to steal the bodies but broke the gravestone instead." He looked at me, and his eyes were wide.

"Really?" I huffed.

"It happens," he said with a pant. "Come on." I realized he was right: a broken tombstone would raise suspicion. The thought sent instant panic through me—what if we'd dropped something, like our IDs or a number? That seemed highly improbable, but the thought stayed in my mind.

Will opened his door and pushed me in, and I had to slide over to the passenger seat. Will hopped in right after me. He drove really fast out of the town, and only when we hit the highway did he slow down. I hastily checked my pockets to make sure the diary hadn't fallen out, and I could feel the pink fur of the journal on my fingertips. Safe and sound, I thought. I couldn't help myself, but I began to laugh hysterically, and I glanced over at my now boyfriend, whose eyes were glued to the road.

"No one will know it was us who were there," I coughed out between my giggles. "Will, we will be fine."

"They'd better not know it was us. This idea was still silly, but now you've got yourself a souvenir," he said through his teeth. I reached over the middle seat and grabbed his hand. I saw a smile appear on his face, which made me smile as well, and I continued to snicker. He still did not find the situation funny.

"They won't, and even if they did suspect that Rupert's body was stolen and decided to check the grave, what would they find?" I asked him.

"What would they find?" he repeated dumbly.

"They would find Rupert's worn-away body; he isn't planning on leaving that grave anytime soon. The worst that would happen is that the gravestone would be replaced." I laughed again.

"I guess you're right."

"I'm always right."

"Haha, yeah right."

"Mr. Grumpy," I teased, trying to lighten the mood. William squeezed my hand and glanced over at me with a smile.

"You're Mr. Grumpy's girlfriend," he said. I instantly enjoyed the sound of that word, girlfriend—that was something I could get used too. We drove in silence for the rest of the way home. By now the moon was completely hidden by the tiny rainclouds, with only the stars providing lights for the earth below.

I saw Ellsberg's lights in the distance.

"Will, can you drop me off at Suria's when we get to town? I left my car there," I said as our fingers intertwined, and I saw Will give a slight nod. I could tell that he was tired; he seemed to blink slower, and little rings formed under his eyes. I couldn't blame him because we still had to get up for school tomorrow, and now it was extremely late for the both of us. It surprised me that he hadn't asked any more questions about the journey tonight; perhaps he didn't want to know, and I was content with that. At that moment, I pictured my parents' faces when I arrived home: they were sitting on the couch in their night clothes, prepared with a long lecture for me. I took a deep sigh and looked out of the truck window, toward the sky. Why hadn't the wolf shown up? What had I done wrong? It had let me down.

Soon William reached town and drove straight to Suria's house. As he pulled into her driveway, he slowly let go of my hand, which I returned back to my lap. I looked at my car, still parked on the empty street. Everybody had probably left Suria's a couple hours ago. Will got out of the truck first and walked around to open my door; his black sweatshirt blended him into the darkness around him. Even when he was tired he acted like a gentleman. He smiled at me, and I could see his deep rich eyes gleam. I smiled to myself. He gently held out his hand for me to take, and I did.

He silently walked me over to my car, still holding my hand. He led me to the driver's door, and I leaned up against the blue Toyota. Will stared into my eyes, and reached for my other hand and squeezed it. We were facing each other, only inches apart, and I caught a whiff of his scent. He leaned forward and kissed me on the forehead, and I instantly felt as if he had left an imprint. My face grew into a smile, and he smiled back. I watched him as he began to walk away, but then he turned quickly, put his hand on my neck and kissed me again on the lips. It had caught me off guard, and I just stared at him, surprised. He tightened his grip on my hands, pulling me closer to him, and then he let go and walked back to his truck. I couldn't help but hope that he would come back again—why not have a few more good-byes? Romeo and Juliet took forever to say good-bye to each other, though that was false advertising because life was not a fairytale, a romantic novel or a movie.

I stood alone on the paved street and felt afraid instantly. How dare somebody leave me outside alone in the middle of the night! I quickly escaped the night and jumped into the car, safe for now. The whole night began to play in my head, and I checked my breast pocket for the little book, which was still there. What a night. The sky was covered in misty clouds that hung dangerously low; soon they would be crying yet again. However, the moon still managed to shine through it all to light the path home.

I drove home slowly in a daze. My mind now shifted onto one thing: the kiss. I had pictured our first kiss in different ways. I must admit that none contained a creepy cemetery, yet nothing could have compared. I grinned to myself as I entered the driveway; I couldn't care now if I got into any trouble because it was so worth it. I glanced at my house, where my parents waited for me. Maybe I could come up with a good excuse, but I had nothing. I stared around as I sat in my parked car, not wanting to leave it quite yet. Something caught my eye: a big figure glowed on the side of the road, and there the wolf stood tall. I glared at him, and this time I couldn't detect how he was feeling; it seemed as though a million emotions ran through him. Why was he still here, at Ellsberg? Why hadn't he followed us to the grave? Didn't he want to be reunited with his beloved Laura? He glared back at me; his head hung low, and his clear green eyes seemed to light everything. I didn't dare leave my car, but I wasn't scared; this creature didn't frighten me as it had before. Something didn't quite fit. I looked down at the diary that lay on my passenger seat.

A huge feeling rushed over me, and I gasped for air. I was being watched again, and the world seem to spin slightly. The wolf held its ground, but the feeling of being watched seemed to be behind me, hidden in the trees. I had always thought that the wolf was the thing that created the feeling, but now I knew it had to be something else, or either the wolf was just really good at what it did. Was there something else out there? The wolf seemed to become aware of my feeling; its ears perked up, he twisted his head in the other direction, and then growling sounds took over the air as the wolf bared its teeth at the being hidden in the forest line. I froze, but I couldn't sit here forever and wait, and I feared that things would only get worse if I stayed any longer. I did the only thing I could and ran for the house door. When I reached my house, I yanked the door open and slammed it behind me. The lights were off and the room was empty. I leaned up against the door, trying to catch my breath from the quick run. Once my heart slowed down, I sneaked downstairs to my room.

"You owe me," I heard Daniel say. He had appeared at my doorway and blocked the entrance to my bedroom.

"Why?"

"You think it's by chance that Mom and Dad didn't notice your late night out?" he asked me with a matter-of-fact tone.

"What did you do?"

"I only saved your behind."

"Seriously?"

"I told them that you went to bed early because you didn't feel well. They didn't even bother to check on you, so they went to bed to."

"Thank you, that was really nice of you," I said.

"One question," he said before heading back to his room. "Where did you go?"

"If you promise not to tell …" I gave a quick look around the room. "I went to Collymed Cemetery."

"You're a weird one; are you sure you're from this family? Why?"

"I wonder the same thing about you: where did your immature personality come from?" I joked and then said, "It's actually a long story."

He ran his fingers through his long hair. "You know, Marissa, you have been acting kinda cuckoo lately." He waved his fingers in a circle by his ear, and I just rolled my eyes.

"Whatever."

"Seriously, woman, don't make me worry about you," Daniel said with a smirk, but I only gave him a weird look before I shut my door on him.

"I'm not immature ..." I heard him say outside the door. "I'm simply awesome and fun."

I rolled my eyes and then directed my attention to my pocket, where the diary lay peacefully. It wouldn't be fair of me to read the diary without Suria; I'd feel guilty. But if I took a quick peak, I was sure she wouldn't mind.

The diary was very small but held a lot of pages. It was worn out, and as I'd noticed earlier, some pages were dirty and ripped. I wanted to open it even more ... so I did. Suria would never know that I read the first few pages.

To Emily-Laura Henderson.

I love you very much, and I hope you enjoy your eighth birthday with this diary I have put together for my baby girl. When you grow old, this diary will bring back memories of your big day and remind you of me. I will always watch you and take care of you. I love you forever and always.

Your Mommy, Laura.

I could feel myself get teary-eyed. Laura died shortly after Emily's tenth birthday, and I could tell that she really loved her daughter. I looked at the front of the diary; in soft, white, fuzzy writing was Emily's name. I couldn't believe I had missed this. I flipped past the first few pages that introduced the alphabet and went to the actual diary entries. Laura must have been teaching her daughter to read at an early age; most pages contained a lot of beginner spelling and words. Eventually it turned into a real diary.

March 2, 1887

Today is my birthday. Mom gave me this book for my birthday. She taught me how to write. I happy to have my mommy. Dad gave me a *big* teddy but he is not happy. He is mad all the time, he drinks a lot of beer. It makes him happy. Today Grandpa came over today too, he told me all his crazy stories. I hope he never leaves me.

I love Mom. She said that a bigger gift will come later. I can't wait to see what it is!

Good-bye

The diary was too sad. I read the first entry over and over again. I couldn't bring my fingers to flip another page without Suria. This diary may hold some answers, and Suria was just as much involved as I was.

I put the diary down and slid it under my bed. It would be safe there. I gently laid my head on my pillow and dazed off into a peaceful sleep. I had the nightmare that night.

Chapter 10

"**M**arissa! Wake up! The hot springs caught on fire this morning!" I heard my mother yell as she shook me awake. I jolted out of bed and ran past my mom without asking any questions. I was still in my red pyjama bottoms and white St. Thomas shirt. Why couldn't I just have a normal peaceful day? Why did something always have to happen?

I flung open the front door and studied the front yard. It looked like it had rained early in the morning. The sky contained white clouds, yet the air was very humid and the smell of rain still lingered. I looked out to the distance toward the creek; a large black cloud of smoke hovered over the hot springs, making it difficult to see the water.

Authorities are down there. Please go see that Suria is okay! Daniel is already on his way.

"Is she okay?" I asked. We both stood at the doorway of the house.

"She is, but you should go down there. It's quite the scene!"

I ran out the door, jumped into my car and made my way to the fire. Suria was probably down there trying to see the mist. I watched as the car sped 20 kilometres per hour above the speed limit. The smoke grew larger and larger until it surrounded me. I parked my car at the entrance.

I slammed the car door and started to run toward the hot springs. Fire trucks and police cars were parked everywhere, and it was hard to manoeuvre myself around them. My eyes darted the area over and over again to try and spot any sign of Suria. The fire blocked out the blue sky, and my lungs felt like they were filled with flames.

I stopped running and stared straight at a large building that blazed with orange vibrant flames. The window sills had either burned to the ground or seemed to be hanging by a thread on the building, and I could hear the inside of the building collapse underneath all the pressure. The beams broke and snapped and fell to the ground, nothing but burnt ash now. The brown building was collapsing piece by piece as it stood on top of the hill. The railings on the stairs were now a molten pile on the ground, no longer visible. The water from the hoses wasn't doing anything for the fire, which continued to grow larger and larger. The grass was no longer its spring green but a dark, ugly brown. Many people stood around or took pictures as the firemen tried to control the situation.

The smell of burned wood overtook the whole forest. The building's roof started to fold in, and within a few seconds it collapsed along with everything else. I now stared at a large pile of burning pieces of everything—wood, metal, plastic and silicon, all melted together.

Colors of red, orange and blue spurted out from the rubble. Firemen started to become impatient as the fire grew larger and larger. It was fascinating to watch as the building that had been there all my life went down in just a few minutes.

A few trees that surrounded the hot springs had also caught on fire. Suria was sitting on the back of a fire truck, with a oxygen mask held up to her face. I quickly ran over to her.

"Suria! Suria!" I yelled as I grew closer. Her face had several dark black patches, and burnt ash covered her blonde hair, making it look brown. She smiled when she saw me; she looked like she had been crying, but her face was hidden under the oxygen mask. A fireman sat next to her and examined her arms and face to see if she had any permanent damage. Her eyes watched me, not even paying attention to the guy who picked up her arm and put some cream on it.

"Are you okay? What were you doing?" I asked in between my puffing.

She lifted the oxygen mask off her face. A few tears ran down her cheeks, and she quickly wiped them and tried to cover it up.

"They got me just in time. I'm going to be okay." She turned her head to face the firemen, for reassurance.

He noticed her watching him.

"Oh yes, dear, you will be fine within the next week. Your skin is just a little burned, and your lungs will recover over time; you got a dangerous amount of smoke in them. Anyway, just put on this lotion." He handed a small white bottle to her. "Apply it on your burns right after you shower."

I exhaled in relief.

A chubby policeman walked up to her. His belt looked on the verge of breaking. "Hello, Miss. We would like to take you to the hospital and get them to take a look at you, as well as ask you some questions about the scene." He attempted to smile at her, but his face remained stern.

"Oh, okay," she replied. Things were awkward now, and the policeman remained standing in front of Suria. He looked as if he didn't know what to say. It was the awkward silence when talking to an adult and getting past all the small talk. After that there was nothing else to say, and I just ended up looking at my feet, thinking we should get out of here!

He spoke after about 30 seconds. "Well, I'm going to check on the fire. Good talking to you." Suria just looked at him and nodded her head. The chubby man then turned to me. "See you around." I hoped not. I just smiled and watched him as he walked toward the destroyed building. The fire seemed to be under control now, but dark smoke had eaten away the blue sky.

"What were you doing here so early?" I asked Suria.

"It's my mom's birthday today, so I thought I would pick her some wildflowers from the Blue, and before I could realize what was happening to me, I smelled smoke and the hot springs were on fire. I was drawn to it in a way …" She paused. "Want to know something weird? I saw the big wolf right before I passed out from the smoke. It just seems to follow me everywhere I go, and I don't know what to do anymore."

"Think he wanted to hurt you?" I asked straight away. The pieces of the puzzle didn't fit anymore. Maybe he was on the bad side after all.

"Maybe." Her eyes darted around the area. I saw another tear fall from her cheek. She must have been so traumatized! I looked around as well for the wolf but didn't see anything. Where could it be? Was it hiding?

"Excuse me, Miss." Someone tapped on my shoulder. I turned around and saw an ambulance driver looking down at me. He had a round face and a little facial hair. "We must take your friend to the hospital now."

I backed away from the white ambulance and watched as Suria got onto the bed. Another guy dressed in white handed her the oxygen mask again. I smiled and waved to her. The doors then closed, and they proceeded to drive off.

I saw William's truck coming up the road; he got out and ran toward me. I stood still, suffering from confusion and shock, as he approached me.

"What happened?" he asked as soon as he reached me. His brown hair was a bit messier then usual and lay in opposite directions. In a way I liked it better.

"The hot springs caught on fire early this morning. Suria happened to be very close to the fire; I think she was in the building, and she passed out. Suria was taken to the hospital just now, but she will be okay."

I watched Will's face as he scanned the area. The place looked terrible; the black smoke still hung low in the air, and firemen worked to put out the last of the flames. A burnt smell still ran through the air.

"Come on, let's go." He tugged on my sleeve. Only then did I remember I was still in my pyjamas. I blushed hard. Will noticed too and started to laugh. "You do seem well dressed for the occasion." I smiled a little.

"Let's go back to my house, and then we can go visit Suria at the hospital." My mind flashed back to her tears that ran down her face. It's reasonable she was crying because she almost got burned, but those seemed to be different tears—perhaps she was crying for a completely different reason. Will grabbed my hand and led me to my car, following me back to my house in his black truck. We soon reached my house and made our way inside. My parents greeted both of us in the living room.

"Hello, William," my dad said.

"How was Suria?" Mom asked me. Will took a step downstairs but still peered into the living room at my parents.

"She's fine; we're going to visit her in the hospital today," I said, and both looked up at me and smiled.

"Well, that's good," my dad said. We gave them one more nod and headed toward the basement.

Will's face was just inches from mine as we sat in the living room downstairs. I couldn't stop myself from smiling, and he couldn't either. He turned over onto his back and asked, "Have you read what was in the diary?"

"Only a little, and I haven't found out too much. But the diary belongs to her daughter, Emily." I turned and faced away from him. "She got the diary on her birthday, and from what I can tell, the mother actually taught the little girl how to write at a young age."

His face was puzzled because he still had no idea what this all was about, but he just gave a minor nod. "Who are these people? How much have you been reading? Is there any reason why this is so important?" His face looked worried.

"Yes. I mean, I think it is important, but I'm actually not sure if this is even necessary."

"I have no idea what you're talking about. Sounds weird, though—a diary in a gravestone? That doesn't happen, or at least this is the first I've heard of it. Maybe we should check all the gravestones for some kind of object," he joked, but I felt that it was not a laughing matter.

"Money, perhaps?" I said halfheartedly.

"Maybe." His face grew stern. "Maybe people will come after us because we stole their possessions."

"Don't worry, it's not like she is going to come and rip the book out from my hands and then start yelling at me for reading her diary. Anyway, she wrote this more than one hundred years ago." His smile grew large, and he nodded. He was completely unaware of the full situation and seemed to think that it was some coincidence. I started playing with his long brown hair, twisting it around my finger.

"Should we read more?" he questioned me.

I shook my head. "But we could read one more page?" I grabbed the book from under my bed and flipped it open to the page I left off at.

Dear Diary,

> **My mom is sick. She told me to not worry, but she cries a lot. She won't tell me why. I don't like seeing her cry. Daddy has not been home for a long time. Mom mentioned something about working on a train. He is always mad. Evil.**

> **Oh well. Grandpa comes today. I can't wait to see him!**

It was barely legible in the condition the diary was in, and I assumed that her mom was not supervising her when she wrote in the diary. I couldn't imagine why her mom would be crying, and if she wouldn't tell the daughter, then there must be some reason other than the sickness. Why was her dad so angry? Was he just an angry person? I looked over at Will, who didn't seem to notice anything too suspicious in the small entry.

Could Rupert have been in denial that his wife had a sickness? Maybe that's why he was angry—that it would soon take her life. Or maybe he could have had the personality of one of those people that when they get sad, it turned to anger. Or some relative of his died? He hated someone on the railroad? His goldfish died?

It would have been funny if his goldfish died, and in my head I could just picture him kneeling over the toilet, shaking it with his hands and yelling "Goldy! Don't die!" And then the fish would die and he would get angry and run around the house yelling, "Come back!" with his hands in the air while he held a beer. Then he would go buy another fish, and repeat.

I started laughing.

"What's so funny?" Will asked me, his eyes staring down at me while I rested my head on his shoulder.

"Oh, sorry, something I just thought of. Let's go visit Suria."

"Yeah, the diary didn't hold very much information because I was expecting some sort of superhuman documentation about saving someone's life." He laughed, and I stared at him in awe. If only he had experienced what I had—if only he had seen the wolf. I thought back to his reasonable ways and how things like this were silly.

He leaned close to me. "Let's go in a few seconds," I said. He moved in closer and gave me a quick kiss. I looked down and blushed hard. In the corner of my eye, I saw Will get off the bed and walk to the doorway.

"Let's go," Will said with a smile and walked upstairs.

"A few seconds is over?" I asked before obediently following him upstairs. He was already at his truck, and I ran out to the passenger door, which he had left open for me.

"Marissa? What's this all about?" he asked finally.

"It's complicated ..." My voice trailed off.

"Tell me."

"Well, this is going to sound crazy." I hesitated. "But there is a ghost following Suria and me. It's a gigantic wolf!"

I soon realized that I could have worded that a thousand times better, but that's all that came out. The expression he made after I said that was completely priceless: his jaw seemed to drop slightly, and his eyes grew inhumanly huge.

"Oh," he said before looked away. "Do I want to be a part of this?"

"The wolf is made out of air and seems to glow," I added.

"Do I want to be a part of this?" he asked again. "It sounds …
rather bizarre."

"I don't know. It's up to you."

He ran his hands through his hair, buying time before he
spoke. "For now, I don't think I do." He gave me a strange look,
and I tried to ignore it.

"It glows," I said, not sure why I said it. Perhaps I thought
it would help. I felt offended that he didn't want to join us in
it—not that I wanted to be involved myself—but it probably
sounded childish to him. We drove in silence until we reached
the hospital.

The walls at the hospital were white and looked like they went
on forever. Suria was eating Jell-O when we entered her room.
She was looking a lot better now, and her arms had bandages on
them. Her face also had some very minor burns. Talk about being
in the wrong place at the wrong time.

"Hey, guys," she said.

"Hey, how are you feeling?" Will asked.

"Very good."

"I was worried about you," I told her as I walked farther into
the room.

"Sorry, ladies, but I'll be right back; I need the bathroom,"
Will said and left the room. I turned to Suria.

"I'm glad he's gone—no offence, but he wouldn't understand
what I have to tell you," Suria said sternly.

"I completely understand. What happened?"

"Like I said a few times before, weird things are happening. I
really don't know how to explain it. How was the graveyard?"

"It didn't work, but you probably knew that already because
you saw the wolf at the fire," I said, glancing at the door again.

"Yeah, I heard the humming the whole time I was there."

"Yeah I think it's bad because …" That's when I noticed
William enter the room. "Because that's why I love white roses."

"Why do you like white roses?" Will asked as he came in and
stood next to me. Suria gave me a look that said, *Now what are
you going to do?*

"Well, because with no color they are prettier than ..." I looked around the room for something to help me and saw a red banner in the hallway. "Red! Yes, red roses."

"All right, then I will remember to give you white roses instead of red. Thanks for the hint," he said sarcastically. Suria snickered under her breath, and I gave her a sharp look.

I stared at the giraffe paintings on the light green walls. After 20 minutes a nurse came into the room and asked us to leave because Suria needed her rest. Suria wouldn't be dismissed from the hospital until early the next morning.

Will dropped me off at my house right after the visit. I waited at the front door until he was gone. A slow, rolling fog started to take over the field that lay in front of me. I watched as the thick, heavy haze clumped together and gently formed the outline of the wolf. It looked angry this time; its eyes were fierce and were a lighter shade of green than I had witnessed before. The creature rose on its back legs with a soft growl and then stomped back down to the ground, making a booming sound. The eyes stared at me even more fiercely, and then it slowly backed up and disappeared with the breeze. I stood for a moment in shock and then ran into the house. Why would that thing be mad? It had followed me home! *Leave me alone*, I thought, *leave me be—quit following me!*

If the ghost wasn't looking for Laura, could the ghost *be* Laura? And now she was just looking for the missing body of her daughter? But the ghost tried to kill Suria today, and from what I knew so far, Laura seemed like a gentle, nice person. It didn't make sense. I needed to find that old man again and get some answers from him.

I went downstairs and ignored Daniel's comments as I walked to my room. I hadn't realized how exhausted I was; the moment my head hit the pillow, I fell into a deep sleep.

Chapter 11

I opened my eyes suddenly, and the feeling of someone watching me was intense. I looked around my room; it was still dark outside, and I guessed it was around three in the morning. A huge glow came from next to my bed. I slowly poked my head over the edge so I could get a better look. The big wolf stood only inches from where I lay, and it had a white glow to it that lit up the whole room; I could see every object in my bedroom. Its eyes were still a light, vivid green and stared right at me, but it didn't seem to blink. The fur on its body wasn't fur but instead looked like moving wind that swirled around like an ocean of waves. The wolf wasn't standing but was in a low crouch, which made it look small. My body froze in complete terror. The wolf stared at me, and then in a flash it turned into nothing but mist and then dissipated into normal air. It was gone, my room darkened and I was alone.

I stayed motionless for the next five minutes before checking to make sure the wolf was really gone. My room grew incredibly cold, and a breeze fluttered through the open window. I could have sworn I had shut the window before going to bed …

I glanced down at the floor where the wolf had once stood. The diary lay in the middle of my floor—not in its usual spot under my bed. The mist wanted the diary! He wanted to prevent us from finding out information. He was the bad guy! My mind wandered back to the feeling of being watched. Why did this feeling and the ghost seem to be two different things? I couldn't get my head around all this—more puzzles seemed to be piling up each day.

I couldn't fall back asleep after that; the feeling of the mist creature still lingered in the air. My back got cold shivers every time I stared at the spot the mist had stood. This was proof that the Henderson family was somehow involved with the mist. I needed to find that old man before anything else happened—before one of us died, or worse, it stalked us forever for no reason. Seconds grew into minutes, minutes grew into hours and I lay there awake and alive.

~~~~~~

For the next few weeks I searched and searched for the old man. I waited for hours at the library for him almost every day. The days flew by, but no sign of him. Some days Suria would join me, but she would get bored and leave, and I'd wait by myself for him to show up. He never showed up. I didn't know where else to look for him. No one had ever seen him since that day when he mentioned Laura and her poem. It seemed the old man just disappeared—gone, poof, abracadabra!

Thanksgiving was on its way, but I didn't count this as a holiday; ever since I was a child, I always thought it was a day where people were allowed to eat everything in sight. We may not admit it to ourselves, but it was true. Halloween had passed quickly, and nothing special had happened. For those couple of days I was a Smurf, Will dressed up as a pirate, Suria was a gingerbread man and Daniel was a pink bunny. I had forgotten about the wolf and life seemed to carry on—but not the normal life I'd had before; it was a pretend life, when things were pushed under a rug and waited for somebody to come by and do the cleaning, but I wasn't ready to grab a broom.

Once the Halloween fuss was over with, I continued to search for the old man. I knew that he had answers, and I had my mind set on finding him. Some days I would drive around the town with Suria just looking for the old man. I had lost many opportunities to hang out with Will because I knew he wasn't interested in figuring out why a ghost lingered around Suria and me. He had never seen the wolf, so for all I knew, he thought that it didn't even exist.

"Marissa, would you like to go for some ice cream today?" Will asked as we sat down in last class.

"Yeah, sure," I replied.

"Or are you still searching for that old man?"

"Will …" I said, but then I ignored his question and leaned toward him. "Come with me tonight; I'll show you the wolf. I'm not crazy, I swear."

"How many times must you 'show' me the wolf?" He continued to write notes.

"Please?" I begged. He still hadn't seen the wolf; it felt as though only Suria and I were allowed to see it. I scratched the back of my head, buying myself a few extra seconds.

Will turned to face me, putting down his pencil. "I just don't …" He grabbed my hand. "I don't want this to take over your life; you're young. Honestly, it's not completely normal for somebody to be seeing a ghost wolf."

"Wait. What if it's not a ghost?" I challenged him.

He raised one eyebrow at me and then grinned. "Then you have an amazing imagination."

"Right." I didn't find this very funny.

"Would you like me to call Ghostbusters?"

I let go of his hand and moved slightly away from him. I felt greatly offended by this. "I wish you wouldn't see this as such a joke!" I hastily grabbed my books and papers and stormed out of the class. Behind me I could hear footsteps chasing me, but not once did I look back. My mind felt cluttered and on the verge of exploding. I began to rub my head as I sped to my car.

"Marissa!" I continued to walk, letting out a grumble every now and then. "Marissa! Stop."

A hand grabbed my shoulder, forcing me to turn. Will stared back at me and put his hands on my shoulders. We stood in the school parking lot as students walked past us to their cars, chatting happily amongst one another.

"I just wish you weren't so busy lately," he said, looking into my eyes. He seemed either angry or frustrated—I couldn't tell.

My eyes drifted down toward the ground. "I know," I muttered. "But I wish you would take me serious as well."

"Listen to yourself!" His voice rose slightly. "You're seeing something that isn't even there! Do you not see how strange this is for me to understand?"

"Imagine being me," I said. He wrapped his hands around my waist and pulled himself closer to me.

"Just be careful." He leaned forward. "Would you consider seeing somebody?" I turned my head, not quite understanding what he meant. He ran his hands through his gelled hair, an action that he did frequently. He understood my confusion and spoke again. "A psychiatrist?"

"I will see somebody," I said. "I'll go find that old man." I still looked at the ground. I tried my best to make this a reasonable statement. He looked down upon me, and I could tell that he wasn't going to ask any more questions.

"Come on," he finally said. I felt his hands let go of me and he backed away. "I'll meet you at the ice cream store around the corner." He pointed weakly before walking away and getting into his truck. I followed him in my car all the way to the ice cream place. Will's truck slowed as it entered the parking lot of Joe's Ice Cream ... and there the old man stood, hunched in the corner with his back facing Will and me. His head slowly turned to my direction as I climbed out of my vehicle.

His face showed no emotion—his eyes were sunken and his lips were pressed in a line. I tried harder to examine his face before he could turn his back on us again. I knew I couldn't leave Will and run down the road to say hi to an old guy whose name I didn't even know. William would be very angry at me for ditching him, but the desire to walk over there grew stronger with each second that passed. Ever since the first meeting, I had always felt drawn to the elder, as if he was the answer to everything. I don't know why I felt this; it was a gut feeling.

I watched the old man as he stood mysteriously on the street corner. His clothes were loose and dark-coloured, just like the first time I had seen him. I wanted with all my might to run up to him and shake answers out of him. He was my only hope now for solving this mystery, and I couldn't stand the thought that the wolf would try to hurt Suria or me. I made my way to Will and into the parlour, but I kept the old man in the corner of my eye the entire time.

Will studied me carefully as I sat across the table from him and licked at my swirl of ice cream. He didn't say anything, so I didn't either. Tension hung in the air like a heavy blanket, engulfing both of us. I could only guess it was because of my lack of interest in him these days, though I still liked him just as much as I did the first day I saw him enter the classroom. I liked his blondish hockey hair that would blow with the wind, and I liked that he always gave me a certain look that drove me absolutely wild. My heart dropped at the idea of ever losing him.

"You seem more distracted now. I'm sorry for what I said. But I think we should be honest with each other, and that's how I feel," he finally said.

"Hmm."

"Just don't let this thing distract you from your life, because what good will come from it?"

"I don't know." *Satisfaction*, I thought, *pure satisfaction*. I licked my ice cream again without making it obvious that I was glancing out the window; the old man still stood there. His clothes were baggy and dark, but not the hobo baggy type, more a "I'm more comfortable and warm with this on" type. Sometimes he would look me dead in the eye, and other times he turned around and faced the other side of the street.

Will checked his watch. "I should probably go. I have a huge test to study for." He started to stand up. I didn't want him to leave just yet; I wanted the tension to go away. I finished my ice cream quickly.

He had already started to walk to his car, and I hurried to catch up with him. I grabbed his red cotton shirt.

"William! Don't be mad at me," I said. I yanked on his shirt, forcing him to turn around. He tilted his head to the side; his hair had grown a lot since he last cut it, and it blew with the wind.

"You never make time for me anymore. I like you a lot, Marissa, and I also want to spend time with you." He didn't dare to make eye contact. I could tell he was hurt—he hadn't done anything wrong. It felt like an arrow piercing my heart, and I couldn't stand to see someone who meant so much to me so hurt. All he did was treat me the way any girl would love to be treated. I was the one who was in the wrong. He was right: this had taken over my life, I was obsessed with the mist wolf and I couldn't deny it to myself anymore.

"I promise. I'm done with the wolf and all that. I swear from this moment on, all my attention will be on you." I tugged on his shirt because I thought it would emphasize my point. The words came out my mouth life like an overflowing cup; I didn't give them a second thought. He stared at me long and hard. It was like going cold turkey—boom, just like that, giving up something I didn't want to give up at all. He read my face, searching for the truth—or a lie. I kept a straight face and grabbed both his hands. Will meant the world to me, even if I didn't show it fully.

"I promise. Please." I sounded pathetic.

His eyes flickered back and forth. Will still stood next to his truck, but everything else seemed to be blurry and far away.

"Okay, challenge accepted. Let's see if you can do this," he said very sternly, but I saw a hidden smile. He pulled me closer to embrace him. I rested my head on his shoulder, and he wrapped his arms around me. I felt really safe with him.

"Instead of going entirely cold turkey, let's aim for a week," I joked.

"A week? That's your challenge? How about two weeks with absolutely nothing, and then we will see."

"Hmmm …" I paused. "Challenge accepted."

"I can't believe that we have to have this conversation and negotiate such things."

"Yeah?" I didn't know what else to say.

"But I really have to go study—that was no joke." Before he entered his truck, he grabbed for me again and pulled me closer for another embrace. To me a hug always seemed to mean a lot more in certain situations, even more than a kiss. He stepped away, and I could still feel the rush of his skin against mine as he got into his truck and drove away. I stood alone in the parking lot, and out of instinct, I searched the area for the old man, but now he had vanished along with everything else I had once believed in. After what felt like hours, I went to my car and drove home.

I got out and ran to my house, heading downstairs and going straight into my room. I pulled the diary out from under my bed. "You're not giving me any answers! You contain very messy writing that I can barely read anymore! This whole thing has done nothing but cause me problems," I shouted at the book. I grabbed the pink fluffy book and shoved it into the bottom shelf of my dresser. There, now it would not bother me again. Out of sight, out of mind.

Suria was now on her own to solve this mess, plus things seemed to happen more to her anyway. I couldn't even decide if there was a case anymore. I didn't know what the wolf wanted at all. At first I thought it was there to help, but now it almost seemed like it was after us. I stared at the closed dresser drawer and felt like I had accomplished something for the first time since this whole thing started. I finally had a great, good-looking boyfriend who really liked me. Why would I want to lose that because I was going insane?

I ran back upstairs and looked out the window. To my surprise I saw the big wolf standing between two parked cars across the street. Its head hung low and its eyes showed sadness. I only stared back and thought, *I don't know what you want or why you're here, but I can't help you.* I knew it couldn't read my thoughts, so I just turned away from it.

The moment I turned away, I felt like I had betrayed everything. I couldn't believe myself. I had just promised Will that I would stop trying to find the old man, stop searching for the ghost and most of all stop helping the ghost. Guilt climbed from my toes to my head. I knew deep down that it had a reason for being here and had shown itself to us, but now I didn't know if I believed that anymore. Things just seemed too complicated.

I wish I hadn't been so caught up in the moment of Will, but his presence always seemed to jumble my mind, sending it in all directions, and it surprised me that I could still get my words right. I wished I hadn't promised him that I would stop everything. I felt as if it all happened for some reason, and now I was throwing it all away. What had I just done? Suria would be even more disappointed in me for ditching her on this whole thing for some guy.

However, I did have another option: I could just carry on with the ghost and keep it a secret from Will. But that was lying to him, and if he found out, what would he do? I had no excuse to get away from it. I couldn't lie to him—what kind of girlfriend would I be? I didn't have the heart to tell Suria either, so I would just have to wait until she brought it up, which I knew for a fact would happen eventually. I had maybe two days before I had to break the news to her. Where had my humanity gone? I was now either a lying machine or friend betrayer.

I tried to get thoughts of the ghost and Suria out of my head once and for all as I lay on my bed. I only wanted to think of Will. I wrapped myself in the bed sheets, creating a safe haven from the world. My thoughts were interrupted by the phone ringing.

"Hello?" My voice croaked from not talking since I had seen Will earlier that day.

"Hello, beautiful, how are you tonight?" Will's voice was cheerful. I couldn't help but smile. I began to fiddle with my homework papers and binders, intending to get some homework done for the night before the long weekend. A breeze blew in through the window, but I could have sworn I'd shut it.

"I'm better now that you called. What's on your mind?"

"That's a very excellent question. Now that we are all good, I was thinking that we should do something very special together."

Guilt washed over me again; I didn't want to drop the ghost case, and now he already wanted to plan something special. I also didn't like how he said "all good"—there must have been a better way to word that. I couldn't handle all this right now, and I shut my eyes tight. I took the phone away and hit it a few times on my head.

"Hello? Are you there?" I heard his voice say.

"Oh, sorry, I'm still here. What did you have in mind?" My ears picked up a foreign sound, something I had never heard before and that wasn't supposed to be there. Someone was outside; I could hear footsteps on the moist ground. Step by step they walked. I heard Will's voice replying to my question, but I wasn't listening—the phone hung by my side as I started to pay close attention to the sound outside, which got louder and louder. Had the window not been open, I wouldn't have heard the person outside. It kinda frightened me, but I supposed it would have frightened anybody.

I jumped out of my bed and ran to the window, which seemed to have opened more in those few seconds, and I found myself looking down at the old man. He glared back up at me, and his face was still stern. I was so shocked to see him there that I let out a faint gasp and backed away from the window. His eyes were watching me as I stared down at him. It seemed as though he was pacing around my front lawn, waiting for something—waiting for me. I didn't know how long he would wait. I had to hurry; this could be my only chance to talk to him. I picked up the phone and slowly put it back up to my ear.

"I'll call you tomorrow, Will, the guy is here!" The words escaped my mouth before I could think twice. Oh no, what did I do? *Click.* He hung up on me. I didn't have time to think about him. My ways were now leaning toward the lying machine, yet the friend betrayal wasn't far behind.

I cautiously chose the floors boards that didn't creak to make sure that way no one would know I had left, especially Mom and Dad. I ran as fast and as silently as I could through the house and made my way to the door. I jumped out the front entrance and down the steps. A few lone stars gleamed in the sky, and a cold breeze blew restlessly. Somebody had once told me a long time ago that stars were holes in the sky where dead people could peek at loved ones. Some people might have found this quote very satisfying, but I thought it was creepy as hell. I stood on the porch and stared at the old man, who stood in the driveway. I took a look around before really noticing him fully. Daniel's truck was parked in the field in front of the house, and my car was parked in the street, just in front of the yard. My parents' vehicle was most likely in the garage. Then I looked the old man right in the eye.

"Why, good day, Miss." His voice was cracked and old. "Beautiful night, it is, a splendid time for a stroll, yes?" He tilted his head toward me. His black hat almost hid his brown eyes, his jeans had small holes and dirt marks on them and his jacket was large and mysterious. I knew going for a walk with the elder wouldn't be the best idea.

"No," I said to him, and his face showed me disappointment and shock. "I mean, I don't know you, and I don't like the dark. I'm sorry."

"Apologies, Miss. Even the wise make mistakes." He looked up at the stars.

"We can still talk because I know that you know something." I regretted what I had just blurted, but I was getting impatient and wanted answers. I *needed* answers.

"Indeed, I do, yes," he replied casually.

"I'm sorry."

"Why?" His eyes watched my face as we stood meters from each other. I could tell that he had something important to say, something that had to be said quietly.

I felt my cheeks turn red a little. "I don't even know your name."

"Yes, Adam is what I am called. Pleasure is mine, Miss. What may I address you as?" He smiled a crooked smile.

"I'm Marissa. You may come up here on the porch." I had two things in mind when I said that last statement. First I noticed he didn't give his last name, so I decided it would be safe not to reveal mine. But even if I had, he already knew where I lived, which was a bit creepy. I didn't know if this guy was good or bad, just like I didn't know if the mist-wolf was good or bad. My second thought was that if he came on the porch and tried anything, I could grab the doorknob and scream as loud as I could into the house, or just run in and lock him out.

I scanned Adam's outfit again; he didn't look like he lived in a cardboard box. He seemed like he had a nice, warm house to return to so that his ancient body wouldn't get cold. He would sip hot chocolate and read an intelligent book each night, filling his mind with knowledge and wisdom. Of course, I didn't know if this was true, or if he even owned a house, but his eyes showed wisdom as he talked.

"Will you tell me now?" I asked, trying to be as casual as him. I hadn't even said what he had to tell me specifically—I just wanted any information.

"Dreams and reality mixed together is a nightmare. No?"

"Excuse me?" I asked.

He turned away from me and looked at the field to the small forest that lay near it. "I know you have had nightmares, yes ... dreams and reality," he repeated.

My mouth was wide open in shock, and I was completely stunned at what he had just said. Did he know about my nightmare, my terrors?

"Sometimes they happen for a reason." He gave me a look that no one had ever given me before. "The terrors you have, you have for a reason. Darkness, lightness, daytime, nighttime—they happen. Apologies for that night; it had to happen. It had to, all to be safe. It had to happen."

"What do you know?" I asked, now stern with anger, not fright. I had no idea what he was saying—he was centuries behind in dialect.

"It's for you to find out, truly." For a second I saw fear in his eyes, but then they relaxed and went back to normal. "Not only you are being watched; I too have to be careful," he said with a warning.

"Why me, though?" I was now frustrated by his answers. Then frustration was powered by anger, sadness and confusion.

He just looked at me with deep warning. He had dark bags under his eyes.

"Please." I tried to say it as nicely as I could, but it came out as more of a desperate plea.

"No." Nis voice was stern and hard. "If I say more, mad he'll be." Adam looked around anxiously. "Two hints I give to you. First: time runs and time is running out fast." Who will be mad? What was my deadline? The fragile man spoke again, cutting me off. "Rain, you see? It is too much."

"It is why I am here? Am I actually involved in this?" I asked. He hesitated, which gave me my answer. So many questions started to build up inside in my head. I had never been more confused in my life.

"I don't understand, though," I continued. "What do you mean, the rain?"

"Understand, Miss," he commanded, and his voice didn't even sound old. Adam took a step away from me, one foot going down to the first step of the porch. The confusion in my head grew as I waited for him to respond, to tell me the second hint. His eyes darted across the street, looking around. He was looking for something—or someone.

He didn't reply until he was satisfied with what he saw.

"Adam, what's the other hint?" I paused as he took in a deep breath. "Please," I begged. I watched his mouth, but then I saw his hand reach out to grab mine. At first I hesitated to take it; I wanted to know what he was going to do first.

His large hand began to unfold the fist that I had formed. My eyes kept glancing up at his face and then down at his old wrinkled hand. His brown eyes only focused on my hand. The corners of his mouth showed a small smile, but beyond the smile was pure fear. I let out a small gasp.

Adam stared hard at me. I didn't know where to look, so I glanced at my hand. In my open palm was a small, folded-up piece of paper—a note. Adam then folded my fingers around the note and dropped his hand from mine. He gave a slight nod as if it would answer all my questions, but I stared blankly back at him.

"You, Miss, are closer than you think," he said, relieved. Then his toned changed, and he was now stressed. "The clock is running out." He slowly turned around and walked a few steps away from me. I couldn't move and just stared at the note.

"Oh, Marissa," he whispered. I looked back up at him as he continued to talk. "Don't judge a book by its cover." He gave a soft wink and slowly made his way farther and farther away from where I stood.

"Wait!" I yelled at him. "What do you know about my nightmare?"

"A test, it was, a test. I'm sorry, my dear," he said. "You succeed, yes."

"What?" I said softly.

"Dreams and reality." He winked. "It may be confused as a nightmare."

I waited until he was completely gone; I didn't understand what had happened. Tears welled in my eyes. *My nightmare involves reality*, I thought. *This explains a little bit.*

I stood alone on the porch for a couple minutes. I opened my palm and stared at the neatly folded paper. I was just about to open it but got distracted by a long, deathly howl that broke the silence of the night. I froze and looked in every direction, clutching the paper in my sweaty hands. The sky was completely dark and full of stars. The street lay lifeless and overcrowded with shadows. Then as quick as I could, I ran into the house so I could read the note in my safe haven.

I leaned my back against the door and started to unfold the letter; tears slowly welled in my eyes and soon I had to hold them back. I tried to block out my fears but they seemed to overflow my body. I looked down at the note and read it.

A Picture Is Worth a Thousand Words.

The note would have made more sense if he had a picture attached to it, but there was nothing else, just those seven words. I didn't understand. I stood up from leaning up against the front door that now blocked me from the outside world. A picture of Will flashed through my mind. Oh no! He was going to be so furious with me. I had promised him cold turkey for two weeks and broke that promise the same day. I was a despicable person.

I stared around the foyer and eventually made my way past the living room to the stairs heading toward my room. There was no sign of my parents, so I figured they must have gone to bed early. My brother sat on the couch watching TV. He must have moved there while I was outside.

"Where have you been?" His head didn't even turn from the TV.

"Upstairs."

"Outside, you mean? And you're scared of the dark. Sounds a bit odd, don't you think?" Now he turned toward me, and that was when he noticed the tears flowing down my cheeks. I collapsed beside him. "What's wrong?" he asked, clearly concerned now.

"I ... I ..." I stuttered. "Had a dream, a nightmare about three years ago. I've never told anyone this before." I stopped talking.

"Then why are you telling me this?" Daniel shifted his weight a little on the couch.

"I need to tell someone, and even though you are a big joker, I think you would understand. It happened three years ago, when I visited our grandparents and you were fishing with dad."

"Yeah, I caught a big one," he said automatically. I narrowed my eyes at him, to show him that I was still busy talking. "So what happened?"

"It's weird." I looked up. "Okay, in the dream—"

"Nightmare," he corrected.

"In my nightmare, for some reason I went outside of Gran and Gramp's cottage, toward the thick, black forest that outlined the cottage. I honestly couldn't see a meter into the forest, it was so dense."

"Yeah?" Daniel reached for the stale peanut butter and jelly sandwich that rested on the glass coffee table.

"Somebody was calling my name, and I couldn't control myself. I went into that forest."

"I can already tell that was a bad idea," he said and gave a nod. I ignored his comment again, but his face showed concern and worry. His eyes were huge, and he rested his head on his right hand.

"There was a man there, just standing in the forest, and I couldn't see his face," I said. "It was like he didn't even have a face—no nose, no eyes, just a black outline of a male." I gave a deep sigh. "He kept calling for me. I followed his lure till I was only inches away from him, and then he did something strange."

"Like?"

"He started to chant—nothing I'd ever heard in my life before. However, I did seem to make out one phrase: 'the power.'" I shifted and sat on my knees. "It seemed as if he was saying that I had some sort of power."

"Is that it?" Daniel took another bite from the old sandwich.

"No. The strange man made a run at me, and he passed straight through me. It was the weirdest feeling I have ever felt. It was terrifying, and the chanting was everywhere; it consumed the air."

"Weird."

"The sense that he gave me ..." I paused. "I felt like I was a different person, a superhero or something. Or maybe it was just the opposite of just that. When I turned to leave the woods, the cottage was gone, and there were only more trees and vines in my way. I was alone with only that sensation with me, and honestly it was terrifying. That's why I can't stand to be alone outside—what if that man comes back?"

"That *is* terrifying," he said. "I don't really know how I can help, but to tell you that it really was just a dream, so keep in mind that it wasn't real."

"I woke up that next day with my boots on. The day before I had this dream, I wasn't allowed outside because it was raining, and my boots would dirty up Gran's house. So when I woke up, I had my boots on, and they were muddy. Explain to me how they were on my feet and muddy, when I never even wore them out the day before?"

"I don't know. Here I thought the boogeyman lived under my bed, but he is actually outside," he said halfheartedly, but I could tell that he was thinking about what I had just said. "All right, I don't know what to tell you."

"You helped by listening," I said. "Answer this other one thing for me: just now I went outside and talked with this old guy."

"Yes?"

"He told me that dreams and reality are often confused as a nightmare. Well, at least that's what I think he said. He spoke ancient gibberish. What do you think he means?"

"Marissa, it worries me that you left the house to talk to him. Dreams and reality? I really don't know. Let me think." He paused for a moment. "Why did you have to talk to him?"

I tried hard to hold back the tears that slowly developed; this was the first time ever that I had told someone my nightmare, and it made the experience feel more real.

I tried to hold it together while he continued. "Usually I don't worry about you, but you've got to tell me what's up."

So I told him. I began with the first night we saw the ghost to promising William I wouldn't get myself more involved in the mystery. Then I explained why I was outside and showed him the note. His dark blue eyes scanned the note over and over again.

"For once in my life, I think I just might be speechless," he said, and he smiled at me. His mind still seemed to be processing all the information. I just nodded and watched as his eyes stared down at the paper. By now I started to feel really tired; my energy just seemed to be drained recently. Daniel hadn't said anything else, and I knew that he probably wouldn't be saying much more tonight. He probably thought I was crazy. If Will didn't believe, why would my own brother?

"Remind me to check that off my bucket list, making you speechless," I said to him. I got up without saying another word and started walking to my bedroom. I had promised myself I wouldn't cry in front of him. I could feel the tears hiding in the back of my head, and slowly they forced themselves to the surface.

"Goodnight," Daniel said as he watched me enter my room. In his hand he still held the slip of paper. I didn't need it, though; the words on the paper weren't that hard to memorize. I crawled into bed and lay motionless. I had all the pieces, but they just didn't fit. It was a puzzle that was the exact same size, but a different picture. Even though I could put them all together, the picture would be ugly, and quite frankly it wouldn't make sense. All I had to do was find the rest of the missing pieces.

One thing I didn't understand was why I felt so propelled to help out a wolf when I didn't even know whether it was good or bad. The old man didn't fit, either; he knew too much. Why didn't he just solve it for me, let it be over and done with?

I drifted off to sleep with those questions running around my head.

Chapter 12

The sky blazed in through my window and created shapes on my floor. The doorbell woke me up from my deep sleep, and I jumped out of bed and ran to the door. I ran past Daniel, who was asleep on the couch, and the TV was still on.

"Daniel, wake up! Someone is here, and Mom and Dad won't like it if they see you asleep on the couch." I shook his leg. His eyes opened, and he took a big stretch followed by a yawn.

"Fine," he said, rubbing his eyes with his hands and sitting up. He reached for the remote and started to flip through the channels. I ran upstairs to find my parents in the kitchen.

"Good morning, Honey," my dad greeted me.

"Hey Mom, hey Dad, who's at the door?" I tried to fake how well I was doing with my "ordinary" teenage life. Mom looked up from the toaster to me, and my dad sat at the kitchen table as he ate his toast.

"I'm not sure, go check," she said. "Oh, Marissa ..." I turned around to face her. "Your dad and I have to go down to your auntie's because she isn't feeling too well. Would you like to join us? She would love to see you. I should probably call her now, actually, and I need to call the bank about those statements, and Daniel's soccer coach needs a call." She grabbed the phone without waiting for my reply.

The doorbell went off again; my dad looked up from his paper and motioned for me to go get it.

"Daniel!" I heard my dad call as I left the room. I didn't bother to listen any longer and went to open the door and saw Suria standing there looking worried. Some of the burns had scarred her left arm, but they were very faint, and I was surprised

111

they didn't look worse; they looked like they had been there for years.

"I've been hearing the humming all day. It has changed, though—it isn't joyful or happy. It is more … stressful and worried. It's even stressing me out!" She was frantic and pulled me outside, making her way to the chairs that sat on the porch. She laid her head in her hands. The mist-wolf was really doing damage to her. Right then I decided it was evil, because if it was good, it wouldn't cause so much pain to someone. Then again, I had caused Will pain, and I hadn't meant to. And if I told Suria that I was going to stop looking for it, then I would hurt her too.

"We are going to the creek right now—the humming is getting happier. I can feel his emotions." She got up and made her way to my car. I headed back into the house to grab my keys, and Daniel stood in the entrance.

"Can I come?" he asked softy, I looked at him and back at the car and Suria, whose face lit up. I nodded. "But I want to drive. Let's take my Jeep." I couldn't believe the nerve of him. Just because I told him about it didn't automatically mean he could join. Suria was already in his Jeep, motioning for me to come join her. I grumpily put my keys on the counter and followed him out the front door, slamming it behind me. I guess Daniel was now part of the mystery, but what were the odds that the ghost would let Daniel see it when Will couldn't? It was supposed to be just me and Suria.

The wind blew on my face as Daniel drove a lot faster than the speed limit; sometimes I thought that he believed he was invincible. My black hair blew into my eyes and swirled around my face, whereas Suria's blonde hair was in a ponytail and stayed neat. The air was cold and dry, a sign that it was going to snow soon. The sun was still on the verge of rising, creating a red haze off into the distance. It must have been about seven in the morning, or earlier perhaps.

The car slowed as we got closer. "The melody, it's … it's getting louder," Suria muttered. I could feel my blood rush as we came to a complete stop. Suria quickly jumped out the car and started to make her way toward the creek. Daniel followed behind her, with me at the back. We walked almost in a straight line until we reached the open grass. I watched Daniel, who looked like he was getting scared. His body would jump every time a twig snapped or a bird chirped. *Little baby,* I thought. *And he is supposed to be the older brother?*

"Hello, are you there?" I said as we stood on the open field. There was no sign of the ghost, but Suria had heard the music from him, so it was close. I searched the trees, and the red glow of the sun peeked in through the gaps of the trees.

"Why isn't it showing itself?" she whispered, disappointment in her voice. I wasn't as disappointed as her because I feared it would hurt us.

"Are you sure you guys aren't just imagining this thing?" Daniel asked. His voice still had worry in it, but he stood tall and brave now. I glared at him, hoping to shush him. I wanted to talk to the wolf, to ask it why it was bothering us, but I supposed it wouldn't be able to answer us.

"We should try communicating with it," Suria suggested, as if she had read my mind. It was for reasons like these that we were best friends. "I'll try talking to it because I can hear it. Is that okay with you guys?" Daniel and I nodded.

"Can you hear me? Can you show yourself to us?" Nothing happened. "Show yourself, please." I had no idea if it could even understand us; would it talk back to us, if it understood at all? Somebody was watching us, though; I could feel it, but for some reason I didn't think it was the wolf. I shuddered at the idea of the figured man out there watching me, so I quickly backed up behind Daniel. Then Suria and Daniel took a few steps closer toward the creek's rushing water, and I reluctantly followed close behind them. We made our way down the bank so we could be by the shallowest part. The creature didn't show itself, and we made our way along the bank, hoping to find some evidence of its presence.

"I have a feeling," she said under her breath, and then she turned to face us. "Is somebody else here?"

"I think so," I muttered.

"The wolf?" Daniel asked. He almost sounded like he didn't believe the story anymore. I glanced over at Suria, and our eyes connected. Did she feel the other presence as well? Could she sense the strange feeling of being watched?

"I don't think so," I stated, "but the wolf must be here. Can you still hear that tune?" I took a couple steps past Daniel and toward Suria.

"Yeah."

Suria stopped in her tracks at two large trees just on the border of the creek bend. I felt more hidden and protected, and my body didn't want to move from its spot. I stared at the small tree that had fallen across the river; if I was light on my feet, I would be able to cross the river on it. Yet my feet remained still. Out of nowhere the woods got really foggy, overtaking the sun, and the air became heavy. I had to take deeper breaths so I could stay calm. It was hard to see what was ahead of me. Daniel, who had been only meters from me, was swallowed in the fog, and Suria was long gone. Shivers ran down my spine.

"It's here," I muttered loud enough for both Daniel and Suria to hear me, but I couldn't see where they were due to the haze. The fog gathered and started to form the wolf, first the eyes and then the very large body. I stepped back, and a branch that stuck out the ground stabbed the back of my leg; I could feel the moist drops of blood flowing down into my sock.

It stood just across the creek from where we stood, and I couldn't help but recall the time it had stood in my room, when our noses could have touched because we were so close. But now the wolf seemed larger and brighter, with more vibrant eyes. It was becoming more real, more alive.

Suria inched closer to the mysterious creature. It didn't flinch at her actions and continued to stare intently at us. The fog swirled all around our bodies.

"What do you want?" Suria asked slowly. The wolf hung its head a bit lower. "Are you here for a particular reason?" His eyes shone more brightly. "Will you tell us why you are here?" The wolf's head looked back toward the ground, sad.

"Whoa," Daniel murmured. "That's demented."

"Daniel!" I scolded. Then I asked the wolf, "What do you want?" The giant wolf ignored my question and continued to stare at us, like we were pieces of meat or something. I took a couple more steps back, away from the intimidating animal.

This was getting us nowhere; we needed more clues. He watched us closely and then slowly made his way closer. I took a step back every time he took a step closer, one time stepping on another sharp twig, and I swore under my breath. The beast seemed like it almost floated on the ground. He started taking small steps toward us again. The frost on the ground remained untouched under the creature's feet. In the corner of my eye I saw Daniel tense up. I couldn't cope with the thought that this didn't happen with Will; nothing, not even fog, had occurred when I was with him.

It still didn't answer Suria's or my questions, but how would it? The sun rose more now, and the light reflected through the wolf. Suria continued to inch closer to the shore. The wolf followed her lead and moved closer to her, and this time I moved closer as well. I looked down at the water that now blocked the two from reaching each other. The creature noticed this also and stopped before its paws touched the water. Suria was just about to put her foot in the water, but something caught her off-guard. A low, growling sound echoed throughout the morning air, carried around the Blue on the winter breeze. The wolf was growling at us; its pointy teeth now showed, and he hung his head lower, ready to strike. The eyes were dark, almost black. The creature lowered its head, and before we could tell what had happened, the wolf pounced over the creek—right in Suria's direction.

"Suria!" I screamed and shut my eyes. A second later, I looked and saw Suria standing in her original spot, unharmed. The gigantic animal had leaped over her.

I spun around to see where it landed, but it had disappeared into thin air. Daniel turned around, looking for it as well. Suria stood speechless, her mouth open and her brown eyes the size of baseballs. I could only imagine that I looked the same. This was the closest we all had ever gotten to the wolf, and it had jumped over us and vanished. A cold rush of air swept over my body, going from the tip of my head to my toes, and just like that, the feeling of being watched disappeared as well.

"Where … ?" That was all I managed.

"I … I don't know," Suria spat out. My eyes scanned the area. The sun had reached higher in the sky and created some faint shadows on the ground, yet there was no sign of the mist-wolf, and the fog had completely disappeared. The Beautiful Blue looked just like it had when we arrived, and no one would have guess that this had just happened.

"Well, I think I just might go jump off a bridge now." Daniel tried to joke, and I watched him make his way to the trail back to his Jeep.

"Daniel," I warned, catching up to him.

"What?" he said as he turned around.

"The humming is gone …" Suria murmured as she walked past us.

"Don't make a joke out of this," I told Daniel.

"Well, this may be just another casual day for you, but quite frankly this doesn't happen to me very often. Big surprise," he said sarcastically and headed back to the Jeep.

"Oh come on, Daniel."

"Okay, I apologize for what I just said, but I am a bit freaked out."

"Oh," I said simply as we got in his car.

"But only a little; I need to keep my manliness." He smiled, but I knew deep down all three of us were completely freaked out and just trying not to show it.

Daniel drove really fast out of the Beautiful Blue. No more words were exchanged; no one dared to say anything else. This didn't help me at all, but it did give me the impression that the wolf was a bad influence on us. My insides felt like they were about to burst right out of me, and my stomach felt sick. I would aim preferably at Daniel and not Suria.

We drove straight to my house. I saw a black truck parked across the street from the house and knew right away it was Will. My heart started doing flip flops. Was it the good butterflies or bad ones? I couldn't tell, but the sickening feeling in my stomach grew. As Daniel pulled up to the house and parked, I saw William standing at our doorstep; he had his arms crossed, and his face was stern. His lips were pressed in a tight line, and his eyes watched me intently as I got out of the Jeep.

The sky seemed to grow darker as I approached him, and dark clouds populated the morning sky. William didn't flinch from his firm gaze, but I could detect hurt or sadness in his eyes. I stopped when I reached him.

"Let's go inside," I heard Daniel whisper to Suria. I heard the side door shut as they entered the house. Will didn't move, so I didn't either.

Then he finally spoke. "We have to talk." He softly grabbed my upper arm and led me off the porch and out of sight from anyone inside. His grip started to release and soon enough he let go. His eyes screamed anger. I fiddled with my hands while glancing down at my red shoes.

"Who was that guy you spoke about last night?" William asked me. His eyes stared right into mine, searching for answers. What guy? Then I remembered what I had said to Will before running out to meet Adam, the old man: "I'll call you tomorrow, the guy's here." Will thought I was cheating! Or worse, he thought I was still obsessed with the mist-wolf—which I was.

"Will, it's not what you think. Adam was outside!" I immediately regretted saying that. I wish I would think before I spoke. Will's eyes grew wide, and he opened his mouth to speak, but I quickly cut him off. "The old man!" I exclaimed. "I'm not cheating on you. Remember that old guy I kept trying to find? He found me!" This wasn't a good answer, either. I looked down and saw Will's fists clench. My body tensed up.

"I thought you were done with all that," he said in almost a whisper. "You promised me that you would stop running after some wolf ghost!" His voice got louder with each word, but he wasn't shouting. I had betrayed his trust all in one day. My legs started to feel very weak, like they couldn't hold my weight anymore. I looked around at something to grab on to, but there was nothing, so I leaned on my right foot, hoping to create stability.

"I … I know," I mumbled, though it didn't help me.

"I've barely seen you these past weeks, and the one night I call you, thinking everything was normal again, you go and ditch me to talk to some old man you barely know. What if he had hurt you? What were you going to do then, Marissa? Didn't you ever learn not to talk to strangers?" I could feel his eyes on me, but I continued to stare at my feet. I had no answers for him. "You're chasing after something that's not even real, and I really didn't want to break it to you because I like you a lot."

"Will …" I started to say, but I couldn't finish my sentence.

"What would I tell your parents?" He cut me off before I could answer. "That's beside the point now—you lied to me."

"I didn't mean to," I protested. "I was going to stop everything, but he showed up at my doorstep, and it was like God handed him to me on a plate."

"Have some responsibility for you actions." He looked away.

"Will …"

"No. I guess I'm just not that important anymore." Sadness ran through his words. "I hoped to never have a conversation like this." I wished he would have been with us earlier; then he would see the importance of the mist-wolf. I looked up at his face, and he remained serious and angry, but his glowing eyes held sadness. I tried to grab him to show him that I was truly sorry for lying to him. He looked at me and then backed up, rejecting my gesture.

We stood silent for a few minutes. I feared to speak more, in case I only made things worse. Will waited for my response, but I had none. Tears began to form in my eyes, and I quickly wiped them away.

"This wasn't supposed to happen," I choked out, and things started to get blurry. I held back my sobs and turned my face away. Will didn't seem to digest what I had said. He turned away and walked to his truck. I stood still, not knowing what to do. I was frozen in that place. He had just gotten into his truck when I started moving, running after him. The vehicle looked bigger and more intimidating now.

I knocked on the glass window. Will looked at me and then rolled it down.

"Please don't ..." I hadn't thought of anything brilliant to say. "You know you don't want to do this. Please," I begged.

"One question." He wasn't looking at me; he looked straight ahead, as if I wasn't even there. But as hard as he could try to hide it, I could tell he was sad. "How long have we been dating?" His gaze remained on the unmoving road.

"A couple months," I sobbed out at him. "Four."

"Not anymore." He turned his head, looked at me and then drove away. I jumped back at the sudden movement of the truck. The engine roared loudly, but it was nothing compared to the noise in my mind, and I watched as his truck vanished down the street. I couldn't feel my legs anymore; my heart ached and tears rolled down my cheeks.

I felt like lying on the road and crying all my tears out. I didn't move for about 10 minutes. Time felt like nothing at the moment. In the distance, a car headed toward me. I ran quickly toward my house, and the moment I entered the door, I dropped down. This was my first real breakup, and it was the worst feeling I had ever felt in my life. My body went uncomfortably numb, and I laid my head in my hands and cried.

"Marissa? You okay?" Suria shook my shoulders, but I couldn't feel her touch.

"It's over," I cried out. "He ended it."

"What? Why?"

"Because I had promised him that I would give up on the wolf and stop running after strangers," I sobbed out. "And spend more time with him."

"You agreed to give up on all this?" She leaned back from our embrace and looked at me, ignoring everything else I had said.

"Well, if it's any consolation, that promise didn't last long." I half smiled at her. "Obviously."

"Well that's selfish of him," she snarled.

"Suria, he is just being reasonable. I honestly don't blame him, and besides, it's our heads that are out of whack," I said.

"I object. Life's more fun this way," she said.

I wiped away some of my dried tears, but my heart still ached as if somebody had stabbed it with a knife.

"You know he's right, though," I said, and this time she remained silent. Her face turned into a frown. She sat down next to me and put her arms around my shoulders. I finally looked up and saw Daniel standing in front of me. He looked shocked, and after a few moments he turned around. This must be really awkward for him; he'd never had a girlfriend. I couldn't blame him for walking away—breakups were hard, and there was nothing he could do to help. I heard his footsteps as he went downstairs to his room.

More tears welled up and streamed down my face. Little drops would run down my face and fall over my lips; the taste of salt overpowered my mouth. Suria's hand rubbed my back as I leaned closer toward her chest.

"It'll be okay," she said over and over. "Don't worry, he'll come back. Boys are the overdramatic ones, not us girls, so don't cry." Suria's voice was uncertain, but it did help, even if she didn't believe it. I rested my head back against the wall.

I sat on the floor for a really long time, and Suria didn't move a muscle. I could tell that her hand was growing tired from rubbing my back for so long, but she didn't stop. I cried and cried until I could not cry anymore. In those moments on the floor all I could think of was the memories Will and I had together—cuddling on the couch, talking on the phone, kissing and everything else.

Suria slowly moved, grabbed my hands and helped me up on my feet. She led me down the stairs and into my bedroom, gently laying me down on my bed. I looked up at her face and mouthed,

"Thank you." I didn't have any more tears to cry; my eyes were dry and hard to blink.

She sat on the bed by my feet. "I'm sorry, I really am. This is a bad time to say this." Her voice was filled with worry. My heart sank—a bad time for what? I nodded my head so she would continue. "In a few days I'm leaving for the farm for the long Thanksgiving weekend, and I have to go home now to help organize the house so we are ready to leave." She stopped for a moment. Her big brown eyes then studied my face, searching for my reaction. "I'd love to bring you along, but I'm not allowed. I already asked my mom and dad."

"That's okay. My parents left for my aunt's house; apparently she is sick," I said as I lay my head on the pillow. "I doubt they would have let me go with you; they prefer I stay home."

She laughed, which was half between a girly giggle and a hyena laugh. "So they can always get ahold of you?"

"You know it."

"You okay, though?"

I smiled at how worried she was for me. "Don't worry. Go home and get your house ready. I'll be fine; I'll just see you in a few days once you return."

Her face still showed worry. "I know, I know. But I want to help you with this. Breakups are really hard." Her eyes darted at the clock by my bed. "Maybe he will bring you a red rose, just to make you angry." She winked, trying to cheer me up.

"Go home. I'll see you tomorrow." I kicked her lightly with my feet. Her eyes seemed to ask me if I was sure. "Yes," I replied, "Now how many times do I have to ask you to leave?" I laughed, trying to brush everything off. "By the way, don't feel alarmed if the next time you see me, I'll be 10 pounds overweight."

She laughed and gave me a wink. "I will call you tonight, or I will come and see you tomorrow morning. And by the way, I can't bring my phone with me to the farm. You know how my family believes that technology has brainwashed teenagers." I nodded, and she slowly got up and walked out my bedroom door. Immediately I felt lonely and wanted her back. More and more memories of William flooded my brain. I glanced over at my window and saw white snowflakes eating away at the blue sky. It made me think of my chequered winter coat, which was stuffed away in the back of my closet.

"I hate breakups," I cried miserably to myself. Soon I was exhausted and fell into a deep sleep.

Chapter 13

I woke up the next morning thinking of nothing, and then his face appeared in my mind. My vision started to go blurry again, and the tears built up in my eyes. I wanted to call him and grabbed for my phone. His name looked so familiar, and his number was engraved in my head. I knew I couldn't just lie in my haven under the sheets and sulk my days away.

I was a free woman, I tried to tell myself. I could now do whatever I wanted and get away with it. I didn't have to worry about some guy all the time, and I could start to party and not have to always dress to impress. These thoughts didn't help me and made me cry harder. I liked dressing for someone and having someone to like.

I slowly rose from my bed and got dressed in my nicest clothes. Some girls dressed up in the fanciest thing they had after a breakup, to show the guy what he was missing; others didn't care and dressed in sweats and a loose T-shirt. The fight replayed in my head, and more tears ran down my eyes. I needed to gain some control, to be powerful, and I would stop crying. I forced away any other thought that tried to overtake me. I crawled back in bed with my clothes on and embraced the warmth once more.

I heard a soft knock at my door and watched it slowly creep open. Daniel stood in my doorway wearing his green muscle shirt and ripped jeans. I'd usually make fun of him for wearing that shirt, but I kept my mouth shut. In his hands was a small box of seashell-shaped chocolates. He walked into my room and sat by my feet.

"Here." He gently set the chocolates on my bed.

"Thanks." I grabbed the chocolates and begun to stuff some into my mouth. I couldn't believe how nice Daniel was being to me. Never had he given me anything except for Christmas and my birthday, and even then it was usually something like a key chain. I pulled the blanket up to my chin and continued to eat chocolates. The sunlight made beams across my floor, and each beam moved in its own patterns. "When are Mom and Dad getting home?"

"I'm pretty sure they will be back tonight, but I'm not positive."

"Thanks again for the chocolates," I said with a smile.

"Well ..." Daniel paused. "I'm craving some eggnog, so I'm going to go out and buy some. Keep your chin up, amiga," He got up off my bed and didn't look back at me. I quickly looked at the clock next to my bed: 1:30 p.m.

I had never slept in so late. I stretched out my legs and sank my toes into the carpet. Suria was going to the farm tomorrow, and I wanted to hang out with her before she left. I grabbed a hat and pulled it over my black hair.

I ran out the door and got into my little white Toyota. My car was messy and had binders and loose papers in the backseat. I threw some of the papers from my passenger seat into the back. I started the car and headed toward Suria's house, but there were none. Some cars passed me as I drove, but I kept my head low and hidden inside my hat. I parked in the driveway and walked up to her white house.

The sky was grey with a few dark clouds, and it rained little by little.

"Hello," said Suria's mom, Michelle. Her hair was abnormally curly and stood out everywhere. "Suria is downstairs." I gave her a quick greeting before I followed the familiar walls toward the steps. The house smelled of cleaning products and muffins; it was soothing.

I slowly opened the door to her bedroom, and the first thing I noticed was a white rose on her pink bed sheets.

"What's with the rose?" I asked. She was facing away from me, and she turned around and, without saying a word, grabbed the flower and put it in my hand. She wore black tights and a long, flowered shirt of all sorts of colors. Usually that wasn't my style, but I couldn't help but admire it on her skinny body. Her hair was neatly done in curls that went down her back.

"It's for you, of course!" She gave me a quick hug. "Are you feeling any better?" Everyone was being so nice to me—perhaps I should date more often just for the breakup sympathy. "Although I do have bad news for you: I'm leaving for the farm tonight instead of tomorrow, but I don't want to leave you because it's a bad time for you."

"Like I said before, Suria, you can go. Will broke up with me because of some ghost, and I've decided that I'm going to figure this mystery out so I know it was worth being dumped over." I had never been more determined in my life than this. It felt good, and I felt powerful.

The corners of her mouth grew into a large smile. "That sounds like a brilliant idea; hopefully you will find out a lot while I'm gone so I have something to look forward to when I come back." She continued to pack her suitcase. I didn't want to hang around too long; her mom wouldn't like that if I made them late.

"Do you get any service out there?" I asked as I examined my delicate rose. It was the whitest shade I had ever seen, with soft pink hidden at its roots. The farm that Suria lived on was like a magical little house surrounded by fields and woods, with numerous flowers that held all sorts of roses, insects and grasses.

"No phone, remember?"

"Oh, right. Well, I only stopped by for a short visit, so that I could tell you that I will be happy and fine while you're gone. I'm just going to avoid Will and go back to normal."

"What about school?" Suria said as she packed her scarf into the black bag.

I hesitated for a moment. "School isn't for a couple days; I'll manage."

Suria gave me a look but said no more. "Okay."

"Yeah, I should probably get going," I said. She gave me another hug and I left.

I had never been more anxious to get home and read more of the diary. My body automatically got itself out the car and headed for the basement. I grabbed the diary from my dresser drawer and flipped to the next page.

> Mommy gave me a dog! He is white, large, cute and mine. But I cannot show Dad, because she says he will be mad. I named him Lupus, and Mom says that he will watch over me like an angel. *Grandpa comes over today. Yay!*

That was all the diary had. The rest of the pages were blank, which wasn't helping me at all. I needed more hints, more clues, more anything! I thought back to what Adam had said: a picture was worth a thousand words. What picture? I needed to find him again. Did this white dog relate to the ghost wolf? I couldn't help but notice that the young girl must have adored her grandfather because she mentioned him in every entry.

I grabbed the diary, the black book from the library that held only one poem and the keys to my car, and I drove just over the speed limit, taking as many shortcuts as I could. Light snow tinkled down from the sky, lightly showering the earth below, but the sky was dark in the east. I ran to the library and yanked the doors open, but they wouldn't budge. I cupped my hands and looked into the dark windows. No lights were on, and the library was empty and silent—it was eerie. I plopped myself down on the white, cracked steps outside the library.

It felt like I had waited on the large, white steps for hours. More clouds covered the sky; every hour they would sink lower to the ground and grow darker. It looked like it was about to rain—it was odd about how much it seemed to be raining lately.

I looked up to see Will's truck pass by, but he didn't even notice me on the steps. Once the truck had passed by, Adam stood on the other side of the road, just like he had popped out of nowhere. He slowly made his way closer to me. He still wore the same clothes as before, and I couldn't help but question this silently to myself.

"Marissa, pleasant surprise to see you." He was casual as usual, but his eyes showed worry and confusion. It almost seemed like he'd expected to see me there—or followed me here. I wouldn't doubt it. I inched myself back, in precaution.

"I don't know what do to," I said as he approached me. I didn't even care that he didn't know what I was talking about. He knew something about everything that was happening. I needed to know more about my nightmare, as well.

"My dear, too hard you're thinking. Use what you know." He sounded like he was almost pleading to me.

"Why don't you just tell me?" I challenged.

"He's nearby." The old man's eye searched the area intently. "I must watch my words."

"What about my nightmare?" I challenged again, getting right to the point.

"Answer this, my dear: What about the dirty boots in the morning?"

I looked at him in shock. "How did you know?"

"I was there." He smiled. "You passed the test."

"What test?" I looked up at his fragile face. What the heck was he talking about? This man was a lunatic. "That was you?"

"Nobody else entered that forest." His voice went into a whisper. "A test of strength, of power."

I had no idea what he was talking about, but he continued to look at me with his heavy eyes. "What power?"

This time, Adam grinned and looked sincere and calm. But the eyes always gave away a person's real emotions, and Adam's eyes showed me that he was afraid—very afraid. "Protect," he answered simply.

"Protect what?" I asked. I started counting the cracks in the cement on the ground. I looked up at him now, and his eyes looked very sad. He tried to smile, but only the one corner of his lips went up, and it didn't last long.

He stuttered but then shook his head. "I must watch my words."

"Why me?" I asked. "Answer that."

"For you see, we needed somebody with real blood, yes?"

"What?"

I looked up at the sky, which was completely black now, and the snow started to fall harder with each passing second. Adam looked up at the sky as well and then gazed back at me. The old man's face looked worried. Cars passed us as we talked on the big library steps, and I looked up at some pigeons that sheltered themselves under a tree.

"I have to go," he said suddenly. "Put the pieces together." His voice drifted off as he looked up at the sky one more time, and then he proceeded to walk away in a hurry. This time I didn't object to his disappearance. He wasn't much help to me these days—just like everything else, I had found. I flipped up the hood on my yellow sweater.

The drive home felt like an eternity. The snowfall had started to form clumps on the ground, and the sky roared in anger at the earth. I didn't bother locking the doors of my car when I got home. I ran straight to my room and grabbed the diary, turning to all the empty pages and studying them. I didn't understand—the little girl hadn't written many entries, but the book was supposed to help me? The pieces of the puzzle had stopped fitting together and had gone completely missing.

I threw the diary hard at the ground. I was getting frustrated, and by now the sky was completely black. I could hear the snow turn to rain, which bounced endlessly off my house. I reached for my laptop and went to the search engine. My mind went blank because I didn't know what to type in. Adam's words played through my mind: "You're thinking too hard. Use what you know."

I started asking myself questions. What did I know? I knew the ghost had shown itself to us for a reason. I knew I was somehow involved and I guessed that Suria was somehow related to Laura. I'd start with easy questions. One question popped up into my head that I hadn't really considered before: Was it a ghost? No, it couldn't be because it didn't seem to fit the description. Than what was it? These questions were simple, but I had no answers.

After a few moments, I entered into the search engine a word that may possibly be what I needed: angel.

Many results showed up, but none seemed to help. Most results contained stories about how angels helped somebody. My eyes scanned down the page, and then something caught my attention on the screen, but it was only an advertising page. The sound of the rain faded to the back of my mind, but it was pounding like a steady drum. More and more stories kept telling me about what angels did and how to search for God. This wasn't what I was looking for.

Then I thought of the poem—it said something about a guardian, so I typed "guarding" in the search engine. I clicked on the first entry and worked my way to the last, but nothing helped me. I kept reading and reading, trying to find one clue.

"Come on, give me answers," I pleaded at the computer.

When I was sure that "guarding" was getting me nowhere, I searched "guardian" and saw a site that caught me off-guard.

Spyrum—Spirit, Angel, Guardian

I clicked on it anxiously.

> A guardian can be many things. Some are different than others. Some are rare and are very special. These guardians are called Spyrums, and they seem to glow and have bright green eyes. They're no normal ghost, and at times they can be just white smoke, or they can form into the shape that they were first created as.

A bell went off in my head, and I continued to read. Why had I thought so hard? The old man was right: the answer lay right in front of me. I continued to read.

A Spyrum has only one shape that it may choose to be; each Spyrum differs from the next. Spyrums can only appear if there is a person with a very pure soul. These people are called Pearls, and they are also very rare. Pearls have very special gifts that allow them to communicate with animals differently than normal human beings. Spyrums are the Pearls' pets, and a Spyrum will do anything to protect and guard its Pearl from any danger. In some cases, a Pearl can choose to hand the gift down to <u>their child,</u> so that the Spyrum will protect the new Pearl. Pearls have protectors that vary, each with a different gifts and parts to play <u>depending on the Pearl.</u>

A Pearl has its enemies, and it will distance itself from the danger. These enemies, known as Rocks, are people who are able to control the weather, and they know that the best weather to kill a Spyrum or its Pearl is in very moist, windy weather, where Rocks can travel through the air more quickly. A Rock gains the power and strength from a Pearl, therefore always seeking more. A Rock is very strong and can never die, only weaken.

If a Spyrum harms its Pearl, it will have to abandon the Pearl for many years as a consequence. If a Pearl is bitten by a Spyrum they will enter an ageless comatose. The number of years it takes for the Pearl to awaken varies; it can range from 100 to 500 years. But note that Spyrums will bring in real- bloods (normal human beings) to help them protect when they are unable to. Real-bloods must prove worthy through the form of a dream. Believers say that the Spyrus can bring even bring back the dead for extra needed help.

Most of the pieces seemed to fit now. I knew what I had to do. I also knew why Adam was anxious. I looked outside and saw that it was snowing heavily.

"Oh no!" I yelled, and I grabbed my keys and ran for the door. The storm overwhelmed me and pushed me sideways. I pushed my fear of the dark aside.

Daniel's Jeep was still gone from the driveway. I climbed into my car as fast as I could. The rain fell hard and lightning danced across the sky. The sky was black, and no one was in sight. The road was covered in water, and I could barely see inches in front of me, as if someone had put a foggy glass over my eyes. I drove faster than I should have, as I usually did, but this time it was different. The little arrow on my speedometer kept rising, and my foot felt heavy against the gas pedal. *Don't slow down, don't slow down,* I thought. I had to hurry before I was too late. The snowstorm smashed against my windshield faster than my windshield wipers could wipe it away. I leaned forward in my seat, trying to see in front of me as my heart began to race faster and faster.

I could feel the car slide underneath me, and the sound of the storm echoed all around. The road was getting more slippery each second. A giant flash of lightning ran across the sky, and I felt my body jerk in surprise. My palms were sweaty and clammy, but I held onto the steering wheel with all my might. It only felt like I had gotten out of bed 10 seconds ago, but the hours flew by, and now it was nighttime. I wished I had eaten something before I left.

I could hear my heart beating at a steady rhythm. I glanced up at the sky: the clouds were moving vigorously, crashing with each other and screaming at the earth. I hoped I was taking the right road; I couldn't see any road signs due to the weather. I continued to drive too fast. The car was losing its grip on the road and started to veer into bigger swerves. I tried to stay calm to keep on the road—I knew any false move would send me into the ditch.

I wasn't ready to face death—not yet, not ever. A shiver ran up my spine again. I needed to stay calm. Breathe in, breathe out, I told my body over and over again. Lightning struck right in front of me, and I flinched again, but to my surprise I didn't swerve off the road. By now my car was fishtailing too often. My hands tightened on the steering wheel, and I looked down at them and noticed they had turned a dark red. The blizzard grew harder and heavier, almost like it was trying to hold my car back from its destination.

Many thoughts clouded my mind, and I tried my best to block them out. I felt suffocated in the car, like the air was trying to block the oxygen from getting in. The car seemed like it was closing in on me, and I turned the heat down, hoping it would help. Breathe in, breathe out. The night swallowed my car whole so that even the heavens wouldn't be able to see me.

The storm grew louder and battered my Toyota. I leaned forward in the seat. Something started to catch my eye, and I squinted to see. Somebody stood in the middle of the road! It was a very faint outline of a body, but it seemed to stand out. I continued to drive toward it, hoping it was only my imagination. I blinked a couple times.

I leaned closer to the windshield. Before I had time to think, a male stood right in front of my speeding car. By reflex I grabbed the steering wheel and turned it as quickly as I could to the right. The car started to glide sideways on the road. I hadn't turned quick enough, and the man didn't move from the road.

A scream escaped my throat, and I shut my eyes right before I hit the man. I waited for the huge thud of a body against my car, but nothing happened. I felt my car turning and spinning on the road, and I opened my eyes. I quickly grabbed the steering wheel, but I didn't have time to think or react. The car was out of control, and when I searched for the man between the spins, there was no one. He had simply disappeared.

Now I couldn't see anything, just the pouring rain. I yanked the wheel to the left, hoping to regain stability. This didn't work—the car started to spin in the other direction. I couldn't see the road anymore because the car was turning too fast. Everything was spinning around me, around my car. Objects blurred together and turned into a black-and-white mush of snow and dark.

My hands left the steering wheel. The last thing I saw was a barbed-wire fence, and the last thing I heard was a high, frantic scream escape my throat.

Chapter 14

I woke up in a daze. The barbed-wire fence in front of me was faint, and the field past it was completely dark. I could feel the dashboard crushing down on my left leg. Something wet drizzled down my face, and I knew it wasn't just sweat or snow. I could see the snow fall down, but it seemed so distant now. My eyes went blurry for a couple seconds, and I hung my head, trying to keep consciousness.

My left leg began to go numb. Pain ran through my body, waking me up from my daze. I looked up at the steering wheel, which was covered in blood. I lifted my hands to my temple and touched the blood that now ran over half my face. I touched my forehead gently, and a scream slowly built up inside me again. I quickly bit down on my lip to prevent it, and I tasted more blood.

I needed help badly. The world started to spin, and I could feel myself slipping away again. I reached for my phone in my pocket, and my fingers wrapped around it, but my hands were too numb to feel it. I swallowed back more tears.

I didn't even know what number I dialled; my vision was still blurred. By now I couldn't feel my leg at all. I lifted the phone to my ear with all the strength that I had and heard the dial tone, so I waited and waited for an answer.

I heard a voice on the other line, and I felt my heart grow warm.

"Daniel ..." I said weakly, only to realize it was his voice mail. Only months ago, he had changed his voicemail to "Hey" and nothing else. I started to weep harder and harder, and I began to dial the house number with dead fingers, but it felt more like I was pushing random bottoms.

I would have called the police, but I doubted that they would believe me: a 16-year-old girl speeding and having delusions of people in the road. I almost feared that they would take me straight to the hospital—and possibly to a ward for the mentally ill.

I waited for somebody to answer the phone. I lifted my head and set it against the cold window. I glanced weakly out the front window. A dark, tall figure stood on the other side of me, and I blinked, trying to focus on who it was. After a few seconds my eyes focused, and standing only five feet away the same man who had stood in the middle of the road only seconds before, the man whom I should have hit. He didn't seem aware of the storm around him. He stared straight at me, and I saw an evil smile come across his face.

He was wearing blue coveralls with a faded shirt underneath. His beard was red and his eyes looked black. I stared at him, too tired to be scared. My eyelids grew heavy, and then a huge gust of wind carried the man away, like he was made out of sand. He was gone. I knew exactly who he was because I had seen him before—Rupert Henderson. I knew exactly what he was—a Rock, and he was on a mission. Tonight was the night to kill. He did die in that fire, but I figured life for him was like the underworld, and eventually the Rock would return, even after dying in the fire, to go after the Pearl.

The soft beeping on my phone informed me that there was no one on the other line. My mind was distant, and focusing on anything was difficult. My leg soon gained back some feeling, and I could feel it throbbing as the pain grew stronger. I looked down faintly at my leg; my pants were ripped and stained red. I reached down painfully and tried to move the dashboard out of the way.

A long scream escaped through my throat once again, and tears swelled in my eyes and started to flow down my face, stinging the wounds. I tried to call my aunt's house for my mom and dad, but no one answered. This storm must have been blocking all reception out of town; I hated that my aunt lived on a farm. I let out a groan. I tried three more times and got the same result. I had only one person left to call, the only person I ever wanted to call.

The phone rang for a few seconds,

"Hello?" His voice was good to hear.

"I need help! I need help, Will!" I screamed into the receiver. Perhaps I should have approached this with a calmer tone, but thinking wasn't an option.

"Calm down now." Will's voice was stern but had a hint of panic. "Who is this?"

"Marissa! I need you now! He's after me!" I was crying hard now, mostly because of shock.

"What? Who's after you?" Now his voice was loud and unsettled. I looked straight ahead of me, my eyes adjusting to what I saw. "Marissa?" William asked, uncertain if it was me. I didn't reply—my focus was now on Rupert, who stood in front of the dented car. A small smile was on his face, and it wasn't a nice one.

"Who?" I heard again

"Come get me!" I screamed in agony as my leg grew more numb. "I'm on the road to Collymed, about 30 minutes in." I tried to stay calm as I watched Rupert, and his dark and violent eyes never left mine. Will's breathing was loud; I could hear him start the engine to his truck. "Hit the guy if you see him!" I screamed, now angry once more. I wasn't even sure Will could understand me now. I hung up the phone and focused my attention back at Rupert, who still smiled. Snow pounded harder and harder, and I squinted so I could see him better. If he stayed here, he wouldn't be able to be with Will as he drove.

Within the next second the storm poured onto him, making little parts of his body disappear each time a drop hit it. He again disappeared as if he was only made of sand, taken away by the wind. My mind flashed back to the article: they preferred moist, windy weather for easier travel. It all made sense. Rupert must have waited for the perfect storm to make his strike, and tonight was a perfect night to attack because it was rainy, snowy and windy. I prayed he wouldn't cause problems for Will. I rested my head against the window, and it felt unbearably cold against my raw skin.

I didn't move my head because I just didn't have any strength to do so. My leg was still jammed under the dashboard. Pain burned through my body like fire with every little move I made. I could feel my breathing grow heavy, and I started sucking in more air to keep my lungs satisfied. The thunder roared at the earth, and I couldn't see anything. I didn't know how Will would find me.

I slowly moved my hand, causing pain to swell in my head, but I tried to ignore it. With all my strength I slammed my palm on the horn, causing a loud honking sound that pierced the storm. I planned to continue to do this for as long as it took for Will to arrive. I felt tears fall down my cheeks, and I couldn't stand to think that he would drive by my car and not see me. What if I died here?

At times I could feel myself pass out for a few minutes, but then I would wake up and start honking again. Lightning flashed brilliantly around me, but I never moved or flinched. I was in too much pain.

I heard a faint tapping sound next to me, and I lifted my swollen head and peered out the window. I saw someone slamming both their hands on the window, but I couldn't hear the sound; it seemed so far away. After some random button pushing, I heard the click of the door unlocking.

The car door that I had been leaning on swung open, and I felt my body fall to the ground. But to my surprise, I didn't hit the ground. I saw two hands wrap around me and slowly lift me back up. I looked up at Will weakly, who didn't show any emotion on his face.

"Oh no," I heard him breathe as his eyes looked down at my leg, "This is not good. I don't want to do this …" He shot a look at me, and my eyes widened in fright. How bad was it? "Maybe I could do something different." He took my face in his hands.

"Look at me. Marissa, I'm going to try lifting the dashboard a bit. Okay?"

I nodded, and he spoke again. "If that doesn't work, I'm going to have to try pulling your leg out. I'll just make a quick call to the police and get an ambulance."

"No!" I yelled while his face was still inches from mine. The police could not get involved in this; everything would turn bad. "It's not that bad," I tried to convince him. I spoke again before he could say anything. "Get me out of the car, please—no police." I tried to act like there was no pain in my leg. He ignored my request and began to dial the three numbers, but I quickly snatched the phone just as he hit the second digit. I hid his phone by my side, and he looked at me in astonishment.

I yelled, "Help me!"

"Marissa, what's going on?" he asked firmly.

"Free. My. Leg," I begged, taking a breath after every word. "Then I'll tell you."

"It hasn't even been 24 hours, and you're already trying to kill yourself," he muttered softly.

"Unbelievable," I muttered. Then again, I would have thought the same if I were in his situation.

He nodded and seemed to forget about the phone as he tried to free my leg. I closed my eyes and heard his soft grunting; the indent lifted a little and I listened for his footsteps to come back to the car door.

"I'm going to count to three." His voice screamed panic and worry. I bit my lip harder as his hands took hold of my leg. "One ... two ... three!" He pulled my leg as gently as he could, but it was still painful. A terrible pain ran through my veins and exploded from my body. My leg was free, though. "It doesn't look broken, nothing too serious ..." William's voice trailed off as he put his arms around me, picked my body up from the seat and carried me into the open rain.

"How's my leg?" I wheezed.

"Not broken," he repeated. "It may need stitches."

His hair was soaking wet, and his face looked more worried than angry. He wrapped his arm around my waist and lifted me partly off the ground to keep pressure off my bad leg. I put my arm on his shoulders and used him for support. Surprisingly the night didn't frighten me, but maybe it was because of Will's presence.

He gently lifted me up and into his truck. I could feel something running down my face, but I couldn't decide if it was blood or water.

Will hopped into the driver seat and looked at me. "Are you crazy?" I looked and him from the passenger seat, and his face was emotionless. Then without saying another word, he started the car and began to turn the car to go back to Ellsberg.

"No! We have to go Collymed!" I screamed at him, on the verge of tears. The tears weren't from the car accident but from fear of what would happen. I held them back with all my might; I couldn't let him see me crying—again.

His face grew fierce, and he was the angriest I had ever seen him be.

"Look at yourself! You need to go to the hospital!" He had now turned back to finding the road.

"No!" I protested. "Even you said it wasn't that bad."

"Do I look like a doctor? Be sensible, Marissa."

"If you turn this vehicle back to Ellsberg, I will jump out of this truck!" I grabbed the door handle and wrapped my hand around it to prove my point. Will stared at me, his eyes wide as he saw my hand around the door handle. He swore under his breath because he knew I was serious, and he slowed down and eventually pulled over to the side of the road.

If I had enough courage to crash my car in a "suicide attempt," then of course I would have the courage to throw myself out of a moving truck. I heard him take a couple of sighs, but I paid no attention to it. I looked over at him and saw him thinking about the whole situation. The throbbing in my leg seemed to settle and decrease, but I felt more blood seep from a cut. William was right, I probably needed stitches.

"Besides, we are closer to Collymed anyway." I hoped I could fool him. He continued to mumble profanities under his breath.

We sat in silence, and the only thing we could hear was the sound of the raging downpour of snow on the roof of the truck. He looked at his hands, which were neatly placed on the steering wheel, and when he turned to face me, I smiled weakly at him.

"Fine." He said it with force. "Why, though? What is so important that it made you crash your car in a snowstorm?"

I kept quiet for a few seconds. I knew it would only make him more upset if I told him the truth. I mumbled slightly, trying to think of an alibi to tell him, but my mind seemed to be washed clean. "I'll show you." That was my answer, that was all I planned on saying. I lifted my hand to my forehead and found another small cut that ran along the side of my face. Will must have noticed me touching my forehead.

"At least let me help you out," he said with a sympathetic tone. He reached into his back seat and pulled out something white. I leaned closer to get a better look and recognized it immediately as his gym shirt. "Put your leg up." He pointed at the middle seat.

I lifted up my sore leg, making sure to guard the slash located on its side. I lay my leg down on the leather seat, biting down on my lip to prevent any minor sound from escaping.

He carefully wrapped the shirt around my bloody and torn leg. I couldn't even tell where the cut was because blood had fully soaked my pants. The formerly white shirt turned a dark red in seconds. I smiled at Will, but he didn't say anything.

"That should help a little bit," he said, and he started to drive the truck again in the direction of Collymed. The sky was velvet black, blocking out the road ahead of us, and Will leaned forward to get a better view. I put my leg down and rested my head on the window sill again. Will leaned even more forward as he rubbed away the last bit of snow on his head.

"Drive careful," I whispered loud enough for him to hear.

"Coming from the master," I heard him grunt back at me. It was silent until I recognized the familiar sign that I had only seen a few months ago. I drifted away with reality and dreams.

Chapter 15

A hand grabbed my shoulder, shaking me awake. I moved my head away from the cold window and looked at Will, wide-eyed. He looked back at me, and his hair lay flat from the snow, yet his green eyes sparkled as he stared at me. Will gave me another slight push, and I knocked his hand away. I moved my soaking wet hair out of my face, tucking it behind my ears.

"We are here," he said softly yet firmly. "Where *must* you go? Where is this place you insisted I take you?"

"Suria's farm," I said. "It's toward the south of town."

"Okay," he said reluctantly. "Just show me when to turn." I heard him mutter, "This is crazy" under his breath, but I pretended not to hear him. I only nodded and pointed William in the direction of Suria's farm. The snow seemed to have lightened up a little. I could tell that Will was still mad with me, but he had listened to my pleas to go to Collymed. The drive to Suria's farm would take about 10 minutes; I couldn't believe all the time I had lost. I cursed Rupert under my breath. Where was he, anyway? Was I too late?

"Here! Turn right here," I told him. The truck slowed, and we began to approach a light pink house that was surrounded by two large barns. The gravel road underneath the truck began to shift and slide, and Will gained control before any bad swerving. He parked the truck right in front of the house, and a large window showed that the TV was on.

I said to him, "I can't walk. Can you just go in and ask for Suria?" He glared at me before very grumpily opening the door and sulking his way to the front door. My night terrors seemed to be lessening, but I guessed it was best to always face one's fears.

I watched as Suria's mom answered the door, her extremely curly hair tied back into a ponytail. I watched as a couple of words were exchanged between them, and Will nodded before leaving. She then shut the door, and Will turned around and put his hands into his pockets.

He climbed into the truck and waited a few seconds before speaking. "Apparently Suria is gone but Michelle has already informed the cops and her husband is out looking already." He was clearly still mad. Lightning flashed once more around us. "Now what?" he said grumpily.

"We go find her." *They won't know where to look* I thought.

Which way did she go? I looked out my window and saw nothing, and then I then looked out Will's window. Something caught my eye—standing just feet away from the truck was Rupert. His red hair stood in many directions, his shaggy beard was a mess, and he still had that same evil smile on his face. I watched as Will turned his head, and then his body tensed. He could see him too!

"Run him over," I whispered. I was dead serious. Will turned his head toward me and then looked back out the window. Rupert was gone, vanishing like he always did, like sand in the wind.

"That way!" I pointed toward the direction where Rupert had stood. "He is trying to hide her!" William looked at me as if I was crazy, and I couldn't blame him. But he followed my orders without any questions and drove down the road. We followed the dirt road for as long as we could. I peered out my window, trying to find some clues as to where he had hidden her. The fields held many hay bales and abandoned houses. It was only a matter of which abandoned house she was in, or if she was even in this field.

It was hard to see much due to the rain. Lightning flashed every now and then, showing me a glimpse of what laid beyond. Thunder roared and shook the whole earth. I continued to stare out at the dark world.

One big lightening flash lit up the entire field ahead of us, and I looked over to see where it struck but instead saw another man. This man had a hunch to him and was a lot shorter than Rupert. His clothes hung loose from him body, like rags draped over a doll. I squinted to get a better look at the man who stood in the field.

"Marissa?" Will said, but I barely heard him. The window got foggy and made things difficult to see. I wiped the window quickly with my hand to make sure the man still stood there.

"Stop!" I yelled at the top of my lungs. Will looked at me again. I raised my eyebrows to show him I was serious. He slowed down and pulled over, the truck sliding a little bit on the soaked road. I threw open the door and without thinking jumped out.

My leg hit the ground, and I fell instantly, screaming in agony. Will was already out of the truck and running toward me.

"Are you mad?" he yelled over the storm. He picked me up and put his arm around my waist. I leaned on him once I was sure he had my body. By now my eyes were soaked with tears along with a mix of snow, but all my sobs were lost in the storm. I stared at the direction of where the other man stood. He was still there, and now I recognized him. It was Adam, the old man! So many questions filled my mind. I looked at Will and pointed in the direction of where Adam stood. Will glanced in the direction I pointed, but Adam was gone.

"Marissa?" Will asked again. I could tell that he wanted answers, but Adam was showing me something, and I didn't have time to answer. I could barely answer the questions rolling inside my own mind.

"Go," was all I managed to say between my sobs. Will looked at me with the same odd expression, but this time he asked no more questions and started slowly making his way into the field. I saw him look back at his truck, but we both knew that he couldn't drive it through the field. The big, barbed-wire fence prevented it.

"I'll show you, I'll prove to you everything. I'll show you," I repeated over and over.

He carried all my weight as he walked to the unknown destination. I looked around trying to see where the old man could have disappeared to. I saw several hay bales and a broken, abandoned shack. Then it hit me—an abandoned shack. He must be there! He caught my attention in front of that old, abandoned shack for a reason.

"Shack, Will. Shack," I spat little words out at a time. The pain in my leg had grown greatly since I fell out the truck. We were now both drenched, and it made our clothes feel 10 times heavier.

Lightning was the only light that showed us where the abandoned house sat. The broken house looked far away from where we stood. It was only a small object across the field, a blurred image in the distance. We walked extra slow because Will carried the weight for both of us.

I prayed that lightning would flash more, giving us the light to see where we needed to go. William repositioned his hand around my waist; it felt good to have his hands around me one last time. I looked around every few seconds to see where Adam was. No sign of him. He must be at that house, he must be! There was nowhere else he could be.

Another light flashed, and Adam's body stood only a few meters from us. I tried to think of how he could be involved in this whole mess, but I couldn't get the pieces together. Will stopped walking once he spotted Adam.

"Go, he's not going to hurt us." I urged him on, but Will was still frozen, filled with complete shock. Eventually, very slowly, he began to move.

"Who was that?" Will uttered.

"Go," I kept urging.

Another light flashed, and I could see Adam's face perfectly for a split second. I wish I hadn't. His face showed worry, anxiety and pain, and those same emotions moved into me. Soon I felt worry, paranoia and panic. I wanted to tell William to move faster, to run if he could. I couldn't do it, though, even if I wanted to; I had already asked too much of him. I started stepping with my good leg, trying to move in time with Will, hoping this would help our progress.

Will didn't seem to notice my attempts. His eyes stared straight ahead, and he seemed to be picking up his pace. After about 10 minutes of progress across the field, he finally spoke. "I need to take a break." His voice sounded weak. He laid me gently on the soft, moist ground, trying hard to keep my bad left leg from touching anything. I started to worry about getting an infection.

The ground was cold and wet underneath my body, but I wasn't expecting anything different. My eyes looked up at Will as he tried to catch his breath, and sudden guilt hit me as he sat on the ground too. His eyes didn't meet mine once. I shouldn't have called him, but he was the only person left. My mom probably would be on the phone if I tried again. Lightning soared through the air again, blinding me.

After a few minutes, William got up and reached for my hand. I took it and we resumed our walk. I repositioned myself against his hip, and slowly he wrapped his hands around me, gripping my side. Will began to move faster than before, and the feeling that I was being watched soon washed over me again. This time it was different because I knew who was watching me—it was Rupert. It had been Rupert all along. I shuddered and searched the long field that held only a few trees, but he was nowhere to be found. I then focused on the shack that lay a bit closer than it did before.

Finally the abandoned house was just meters from us.

The shack was made out of wood, but some beams had fallen, and there were holes in the side. The night sky seemed to consume it completely. Will reached the doorway of the shack, still holding me up. Half the roof was missing, and most of the old, cracked cement floor was wet. The shack had three windows, but either they were broken or a wooden beam blocking the view to the outside.

Strangely the door was missing, so Will leaned himself and me up against the inside wall. I looked inside the shack to see nothing, just darkness. I wanted to cry again and again because I worried that I was too late.

Chapter 16

"Who's there?" A familiar voice asked from the darkest corner." William tensed up and then slowly began to move toward the corner. Through the darkness two large green eyes shone, lighting up the whole shack. Will put me down close to the door, and I put my hands out so I knew where the floor was. I blinked a few times as I stared toward the green eyes, waiting for my sight to adjust to the sudden brightness. Then it came into view, and I couldn't believe what I was seeing.

Suria lay on the shack's hard, wooden floor in Daniel's arms—with the wolf lying on the ground just next to them. It just didn't make sense. I didn't know why Daniel was here. I knew Adam was involved somehow, but I couldn't think of the reason. I looked carefully at Suria and noticed that she lay lifeless on the floor, her eyes closed. In horror I searched Daniel's face, and it looked like he had been crying. He wiped his eyes over and over again. "Marissa?" he asked. I nodded.

"Why are you here, Daniel?" I watched him, but from the corner of my eye I watched the wolf too. Its green eyes showed delight that we were here, but it also showed fear.

"Well, while I was getting eggnog, this old man came up to me and told me that they needed another real blood. At first I thought it was a joke and laughed, so I continued to speak with him."

"And ... ?" I choked out.

"The old man told me that Suria was in trouble. I swear that I tried to call you, but the storm must have interfered. I came out here to check on her."

He is such a lovesick puppy, I thought. Will slowly crept closer to Suria to see whether she was still breathing, and the wolf watched him very carefully. "She's not dead, she is just knocked out," Daniel answered my unspoken question. Relief ran through my whole body; I couldn't stand to lose my best friend. Will touched her face; his cold hand must have shocked her body because in a blink, her eyes were wide open and terrified.

"What's happening?" Her big brown eyes searched the room and rested on each face, trying to recall what had happened to her. I slowly dragged myself toward her so I could explain.

"The wolf that had been following us this entire time is a Spyrum, which is some sort of guardian. His name is Lupus, and you are something called a Pearl. One hundred eighteen years ago, you were that little girl named Emily, the one who owned the diary," I said in a hurry, and I watched her face as a tear ran down it. I had to hurry with what I said—the sooner she processed the information, the safer we all were.

William turned to me, his mouth wide open, and he glared at me in shock. I knew somehow that he finally believed me, believed everything. I carried on speaking, "Remember Rupert?" I asked Suria, who hadn't spoken a word. "He tried to kill you with a fire. But … but Lupus must have dragged your body away." A couple more pieces fell into the puzzle. Those scars on her arm weren't from the fire; they were from the wolf's teeth dragging her.

"Why am I still alive?" Suria's voice sounded distant.

"The Spyrum guardian thing had to bite you so you wouldn't die in the fire, but he was forced to leave you for a hundred years as a consequence, because a Spyrum shouldn't bite its Pearl." Something flashed in the corner of my eye, and I quickly turned my head to see Adam.

"Hello, Marissa, my dear. It's good to know you figured it all out. The clock hands run short, my dear. Rupert will shortly appear to finish the job, to finish off my precious Emily." I noticed he used her old name.

"Lupus," Suria mouthed and looked at the wolf. They lived among the stars, I recalled from the poem—Lupus was a constellation. My mind finally arrived at limited questions.

I was still on the opposite side from Suria, and I feared that the wound in my leg would split open if I moved more. Will seemed to notice this, and he walked back to me and stood next to me. I could feel his touch against mine and rested all my weight onto his side, yet he still managed to keep his stance strong and postured.

"Well, isn't this a pleasant surprise." The deep voice came from behind me. I turned around and looked at the doorway. Rupert stood tall, and his voice was hard and cold. His eyes shifted toward Suria, who sat in the corner with the glowing dog. Suria's eyes were wide as she stared at the man who was her father. The old shack creaked at every small movement.

"Suria! You must understand all this! Lupus has returned for you," I cried through my tears. She just needed to understand. "Lupus is here to claim you again! You are his and he is yours!" I could barely understand what I was saying; I bet nobody could. I didn't care—I had to get my point across.

Rupert took a couple steps into the broken residence. "The fire was a brilliant idea. It was fool-proof, except that damn pet of yours got in the way." Rupert looked directly at Suria, who still stared back at him in shock.

"Don't say that!" she screamed.

"You see, I cannot die. However, I must take time to regain all my strength after I die." He began to laugh uncontrollably. It was an evil, high-pitched squeal, and I couldn't help but imagine him as some sort of pig. "I never died in that fire, and whenever I kill a Pearl, I regain all my power and come back even stronger."

Suria stared and her mouth hung open. I looked around. Everyone now stood in the little abandoned house: Suria, Daniel and Lupus in one corner; me and Will opposite them; Adam in the middle of the commotion and Rupert at the broken doorway.

"You are not going to touch her. I have been out to kill you ever since you killed my little girl, Laura. You poisoned her! My beautiful girl died suffering!" Adam yelled angrily. He moved himself in front of Suria—or Emily; I didn't know which to call her, but now I understood how Adam was connected in all this. That crazy old guy from the library was Suria's grandfather. In the article it had said that the wolf would get others involved, and it had brought Adam back to guide Suria because Lupus couldn't while it had to leave Suria alone. That's why I was involved, too. Suria's body went invisible for those 118 years, and then someone found her and that was why she couldn't remember her past. I always forgot she was adopted.

Rupert gave a little chuckle. "You really think so? I'm going to kill her, and I'm going to do it with joy." Then he charged at Adam. Rupert's strength was incredible powerful. He seemed to have the strength of an immense bear! How many Pearls had he killed up to this point?

Lupus jumped up just as Adam and Rupert collided with each other, and the wolf began to bite deep wounds in Rupert's ghostly leg. Adam threw Rupert a punch in the face but Rupert remained untouched. He was so strong, a punch like that left him unaffected. Adam and Lupus charged after him but Rupert dodged the attack. Rupert threw a frantic punch at the wolf's face, which made it back up. Rupert kept all his focus on the white wolf. I watched in amazement because I knew I couldn't help … yet.

Adam tried to push Rupert farther and farther away from the shack, but Rupert's dark eyes grew angrier, and he hit the old man and made him crash to the ground.

"It's sad, you know," Rupert said as he looked down at Adam. "I killed your daughter, but she had already passed the gift to our daughter. I hadn't even thought of that. I guess killing Laura did nothing!" He laughed, and I studied Adam's face, unable to tell what emotion was going through him. "And you know what's even funnier? I'm going to kill you again. It was the perfect murder, but that stupid wolf had the idea to bring you back." He laughed harder and harder. "Was that your great idea? Give the Protect Power to that girl after Lupus brought you back? Just so she could hide Emily from me all these years? You knew I would find her. Shadowing her was completely idiotic." Rupert carried on, purposely toying with Adam. I realized that when he said "that girl," he meant me. I had the Protect Power.

Lupus's large figure jumped out of nowhere and Rupert quickly grabbed me as a human shield. In that split second, Lupus changed his course of attack midair therefore landing awkwardly on his front paws. Rupert had his grip around my neck and shoulders and I could feel bruises begin to swell. I quickly clawed at the hands that touched my body, trying anything to free myself. Suddenly I felt myself on the ground and a jolt of pain elapsed around my hurt leg. I held back a scream and grunted instead.

Rupert stood tall above me and something shiny was hidden in his right hand. A knife I thought. The blade of the knife was pointed toward the wolf, who had barely regained his stance. The wolf bared its teeth and a long growl echoed around me. My mind blanked but my body reacted.

One moment I'm lying on the ground and the next I'm on Rupert's back. I wrapped my hands around his neck as tightly as I could. He swung the knife at me but I quickly dodged the blade. I had taken him by surprise and he hadn't had time to think. I knew what I had to do--- get the knife out of his hand. Everything seemed to happen in slow motion. I watched as he reached behind him and flipped me over his shoulders—as if I were a parasite on his body. I landed directly between Lupus and Rupert but I felt no pain. None. My leg seemed to stop hurting and the blood on my face vanished. I never felt the impact on the ground or heard the screams in the shack. Adrenaline blocked all other senses. The only noise that I heard was the 'cling' of sharp metal falling to the ground.

I knew what I had to do, as if it were written instructions. Knife, Marissa I thought. Perhaps my Protect Power was an advantage to me. The vanished pain in my body was slowly returning but I brushed it aside. A flicker of light caught my attention. The dagger lay just a foot away from me and I instantly reached and grabbed it. With all my strength, I pushed off my good leg with the dagger in hand. I jumped directly at Rupert. He swung his fist at me but was too late. The dagger landed flawlessly in his chest and he staggered backward, caught off guard. I fell back to the ground, the pain re-introduced. Rupert glared at me with pure hatred. He hastily pulled the blade out and held it above me.

"Kill me! I dare you!" I challenged. I shut my eyes as the blade came toward me.

But nothing happened. Was I dead? I opened my eyes and everything was black. I couldn't hear or see anything. Then my vision focused and I was back in the shack but no sign of Rupert. Lupus stood next to me--- a knife wound in his shoulder. He stood tall and focused on something across the room. I followed his gaze and saw that Rupert stood by the doorway, holding his hand over the injury. That's when Lupus charged at Rupert.

Adam still lay on the dirty grass, not moving. Will was by his side now.

"Will!" I yelled at him. "Is he okay?" Adam's head turned toward me, and he gave a quick nod.

"Get up!" I yelled at him. "Get up now, Adam! Don't let him win." Adam's head turned toward me, and he gave a quick nod before he got up.

I turned my attention back to Rupert and Lupus's fight; they were a bit farther from the shed but still within viewing distance. I watched as Rupert picked up Lupus and threw him to the ground. Each was badly wounded. I turned my attention back to Lupus. His green eyes were hidden, and his light slowly faded from his furry body. But I knew that Rupert may be very powerful, Lupus could take him on. Rupert had been badly hurt, he seemed to be staggering instead of walking, and he was weak. Both were hurt badly, the fight could go either way now. Lupus was large and vicious but Rupert was strong … very strong.

"No!" I heard Suria cry. I looked back to see Daniel preventing her from running to Lupus. "Please, no! Get up, Lupus! For Laura! Do it for my mother!" She fell on her knees and started to cry into her hands. Her long, curly blonde hair hung over her face.

I looked back and couldn't see Rupert or Lupus anywhere. Had I helped? *Come on, Lupus* I urged on in my head. *Do it for*

Laura, who died because of him. I looked up at Will's face; he mouthed the word "Sorry."

Strangely, I wasn't afraid of anything.

"Do you ungrateful teenagers want to know what's even funnier?" Rupert's evil voice came from the broken doorway. "I'm going to kill the rest of you for my own pleasure!" He walked past me and toward Suria. His wound badly bleeding yet he still stood great.

I looked behind him at the doorway to see that Lupus's body wasn't there anymore. My emotions ran wild, and I didn't know what to think of this; it could be good or bad. *Please no*, I begged again in my head. Suria's cries echoed through the walls of the old shed. I looked back to see Rupert reaching for her face.

"Don't touch me!" she screamed at him. "You murderer!" But the comments didn't stop him. "You monster!" He held her face with both his hands and slowly knelt down in front of her.

"If I knew you would have been so beautiful, maybe I wouldn't have killed you. Sorry, Dear, I have to do what I have to do. I'm going to be powerful, very powerful—all thanks to you. You are my gateway to the all power." Then Rupert mocked her. "Think of this as helping your dear old father." I could even picture his evil smile on him as he was looking at her. His back still faced Will and me.

"You will not touch her!" I yelled. I was half standing, half sitting but I felt powerful inside. I felt almost invincible. Lupus charged through the shack walls and attacked Rupert, forcing them out the other side.

Whoa I stabbed somebody, I thought. If I hadn't done what I did, Rupert would have been too strong.

Suria lay in the corner with Daniel. Daniel than backed up into the corner, and that was when I realized the reason he was here. Adam thought I had given up on the wolf, which made him go for the next best person to bring into this to help. Suria wasn't human—I mean, she was when she was Emily, but ever since she'd been bitten by the wolf, she wasn't a true human being. Though Daniel was a real-blood, I still possessed the Protect

Power. My mind slowly formed all the missing pieces together. Only Will, Daniel and I were real blood. The others either were a guardian, dead or evil.

I looked around and out the broken doorway. No sign of Rupert or Lupus. I started to shake; I couldn't stand not knowing what was happening with them. The snowflakes poured down through the broken ceiling. Lightning flashed high in the sky and were followed by the roar of thunder. Only now did I realize how cold it was outside, the hairs on my body stood up as chills ran from my head to my toes.

"Good job," Will mouthed at me. He was still attending to Adam. I looked down at my leg, totally forgetting the pain that once was there. I needed to get to a doctor.

I began counting small, melted snowflakes that fell from the sky. I wasn't scared of the night anymore. We had won, I could tell. I had stabbed Rupert directly in the heart. He wouldn't die though--- he would never die. He would only weaken. What if he returned in the future for revenge....?

I continued counting, five … six … seven …

A scream echoed from outside the building; it was a man's scream. Everyone was now at full attention and looked around anxiously. I tried to sneak a look outside the doorway. I could hear flesh tearing.

Everything grew silent and Lupus walked through the door. It had only been a minute that they were gone. The sound of torn flesh hung fresh in my memory. Adam weakly got up and joined Suria in the corner. I watched her body soon become ghost-like, glowing.

I watched as Adam helped Suria up, and she gave him a big hug. Lupus also stood and made its way towards them, tail wagging. "My love, it's good to have you back," I heard Adam whisper in her ear.

Suria's skin started to radiate like Lupus's and Adam's. Her skin shone brightly, and the room got lighter. The storm was nothing but an echo in the back of my mind. I zipped up my hoodie because the night had grown ice cold.

All three of them glowed now, and their skin was milky white. I saw Daniel from the corner of my eye, and he walked over to where Will and I laid. He crouched down and looked down at the dust on the floor. Will still watched the scenario unfolding in the middle of the old shack. Daniel looked over at me, and we shared a glance.

The wolf, Adam and Suria turned to us. Will helped me get up, and we approached them, with Daniel just a few steps behind. I couldn't believe my fun brother was now so sad because the girl he loved would most likely be leaving. He didn't look up once; I tried walking in step with William again to get us to Suria faster. The whole shack began to grow lighter.

"I get to go home," Suria said, and tears ran down her white cheeks. "I get to meet my mom again. I get to be free. I ..." She looked down. "I don't want to leave you three. When I was little I wanted to die, I wanted to leave. You stopped me." Her big brown eyes started to sparkle. "I couldn't have done this without you."

I smiled weakly. "Don't go."

"Tell my family I love them," she said with a smile.

I looked down at my feet. "Don't leave me, please, Suria. You were my best friend that I did everything with, and no one can replace you." Tears started to run down my face, and the ground got blurry. "I don't know what I am going to do without you. I need you." I looked back up at her.

She made her way toward me and put her glowing hand on my face. "I'll always be with you, no matter if I'm here or if I'm gone. We are always going to be best friends." She backed up. Her voice softened.

More tears fell from my eyes. *No, Suria, please don't*, I begged silently. She moved herself closer and I embraced her.

I cried hard into her shoulder as she embraced me for the last time. "Forever and always best friends," I whispered. We released each other, and her eyes shone brightly and were glassy, but she had no tears. I couldn't control my tears; my heart broke in two and then slowly shattered into tinier pieces. Losing her like this felt worse than death. I realized that the girl I loved, laughed with and shared everything with would be leaving me.

"Forever." She backed up and looked at Will. "You take care of her for me, William." He gave a quick nod and then stepped forward for a good-bye hug. I absorbed the last moments of her, of her wavy blonde hair, her beautiful brown eyes.

"I will," he said once they were finished hugging.

Then Suria's glowing body turned to Daniel, and she made her way in front of him. Her eyes looked into mine, and I gave a quick nod. "I'll miss you, Daniel."

He looked long and hard at her face, and his eyes began to tear up. He fought hard to not show, but soon his resolve burst and the tears flowed. She stepped in even closer until their bodies were touching. Her face moved closer to his and gave him a kiss that he had been waiting for a long time. I watched as his eyes grew large and he wrapped his arms around her body. "Please," he whispered.

She gave him another kiss on the cheek and backed up.

"'Bye," she said very gently, like an angel. A glowing Pearl she was.

"I'll miss you too, Suria," he said once they were done, and his blue eyes were watery. "I'll miss you," he repeated under his breath. Suria backed up and went to stand with Adam and Lupus, but she glanced back at me, and I could tell the tears were coming now.

"I get to meet my mom," she said again excitedly. "But I have to leave someone I love." She ran back to me and gave me another long hug. "I couldn't leave without one last hug." She smiled and then went back to Adam.

"Thank you, everyone, especially you, Marissa, my dear," Adam said, and he then turned and looked back as if to add something.

"Adam?" I looked at him. "What is the Protect Power exactly?"

The elderly man smiled, revealing all his wrinkles. "My dear, this question I did expect."

"So?" I urged him on.

"The nightmare, yes? It was neither a nightmare nor a dream—it was reality. Understand? The Protect Power is a very rare gift among real bloods. It means you have the power to hide and shadow the Pearls," Adam said. I turned my head slightly, not fully understanding. He continued to speak. "That night when you were brought forward into the forest? Nobody else would have done that, except you. You accepted the Protect Power.

"Why did it terrify me for my whole life!" I blurted out.

"Ah, my dear, the Protect Power affects each one differently. It scared you for the right reasons—to protect you and my granddaughter." He put his hand on Suria. I quickly thought back to the times where my fear of the night had saved me. My mind flashed back to the night when I stood in front of my house door but didn't open it. What would have happened to me if I had?

"Wait," I said. "How did I protect her?"

"Every time you were with Emily, he couldn't find her." Adam said. That explained why he had found her walking home from the store, or when the hot springs caught on fire.

"Okay," was all I said. I was completely speechless

Adam had a grin on his face, but he didn't show his teeth and then stepped back with the other ghosts. Lupus gave a long howl, and in a flash with the lightning, they were gone.

"I hope to see you soon," I heard Suria say before she left.

We now stood in the complete darkness. The only thing we could hear was the sound of the snow hitting the remains of the roof. My body was cold and soaked, and I started to shiver badly. The tears kept rolling down my cheeks as I leaned up against Will. I held the rose close to my body as it glowed; it was the only thing I had left of my friend. At that instant, I realized I wasn't afraid anymore—of anything.

Then it hit me. I had lost my best friend, I just witnessed a huge fight, I got into a car accident, my leg was hurt, I stabbed someone and my face was bleeding. My mind flashed back again: Rupert was always watching—he had tried to drown me, burned the hot springs down to kill Suria, was at the creek when Lupus growled at us and caused my car accident. My heart skipped a beat at all of this. He had tried to stop us since the beginning, but I had created a difficulty in his plans. Me.

It was all too much. I felt so alone and afraid. I started to feel lightheaded, and the room began to spin. I felt my body collapse, and the last thing I saw was the floor.

Chapter 17

I opened my eyes and scanned the room. White bed sheets, funny smells and cheesy wallpaper. It took me two seconds to realize I was in the hospital. I sat up and realized I couldn't feel my leg, and I quickly glanced down and saw it was wrapped in a pale bandage. I noticed some signatures were already on it, but I didn't try to read them.

My head started to throb, and I lifted my hand and touched my forehead. A huge line of stitches went across my forehead and to the right side of my face. I managed to feel seven stitches. I heard faint snoring coming from the side of the room and saw my parents sleeping in the armchairs that sat neatly on each side of a little blue table.

"Mom? Dad?" I whispered, my throat hurt too much to speak louder. They didn't flinch when I called their names. I took a deep breath and began to speak louder.

"Mom! Dad!" I tried to shout. It hurt my throat even more, but it did the job. My mom's eyes opened, and in a second she was kissing my cheeks and forehead.

"It's so good that you are okay!" More hugs and kisses. "I promise I'll never leave the house ever again without you."

I looked at my dad with pleading eyes to free me, and he did. "That's enough now, darling, now tell us everything that happened." I nodded and smiled sweetly. My story was short and sweet; I told them that Daniel and I had gone to visit Suria but she wasn't home so we had left. However I had crashed the car and I could only get in contact with Will, therefore he picked me up. I couldn't tell them much more without sounding crazy. This was an adventure not meant for everyone.

Epilogue

Three Months Later

It was now close to February, and I had experienced my first snowmelt without my best friend. I still thought of Suria every day. In the past three months I had cried myself to sleep every night without her by my side. Tears ran down my face as I thought of all the times we had together, and all the times we would miss out on.

"Marissa, there is a visitor for you; I sent him to your room!" my mom shouted down at me. I looked at my door waiting for it to open. I listened and heard soft footsteps making their way to me, and then the door opened slightly.

"Marissa?" Will said, and then his face found mine. "Please don't be upset." I tried not to be. He sat down next to me and gave me a quick kiss. I knew then that everything would be okay.

That day in the hospital, my mom told me some bad news: that Suria went missing in the storm and investigators were still looking for her. But I knew that they will never find her.

"Marissa," Will said, and then he paused. "I promised a good friend of mine that I would take good care of you. And I will do my utmost to do everything your heart desires. Losing a friend is hard; you will never forget her." He smiled and leaned closer, and our noses touched. He put a black bag down on my floor.

"Thank you," I whispered. I slowly put my arms around his neck and pulled his head in for a long kiss. Once we released each other, we sat there in silence. No words needed to be spoken.

My mind wandered back to Suria, and I knew I wouldn't forget her. I could feel that she would take care of me, and that

Lupus would watch over us down here. Some days I swore I could feel her near me or hear her voice in my mind.

Will grabbed my hand and squeezed it. "Oh, I almost forgot." He reached into the bag that he had thrown on the floor. When he turned back to face me, he was holding a snow-white coloured rose. It instantly took my breath away.

"Thank you," I breathed. I grabbed the rose and laid it gently on my dresser, right next to the wilted flower that Suria had given me.

I heard another knock at my door, and both Will and I looked to see who was there.

"Can I come in?" Daniel entered and sat down beside me. "I can't stop thinking about her. One day, I will see her again." I nodded to reassure him as I looked up at the white rose sparkling next to my bed.

And maybe he would see her; the future was too undetermined. No one knew what they would be doing in 10 years and who they would know and who they would have lost. But one thought that stuck in my mind was that Suria was with her family, her real family, and I hoped that one day, I too would see her again. I liked to think that she had moved on to the other world, to heaven. She had needed Lupus and Adam because they helped her face the reality of death.

About the Authors

Dané and Julie le Roux were born on March 2, 1995, in Kimberly, South Africa. Even as young children, they showed interest in creating stories and using their imaginations. At the time of this book's publication, they live in British Columbia, Canada. Good news to readers who enjoyed this book is that another book by the twins (not a sequel) will soon be published. For more information, questions and comments you have about the book, please email us:

d.j.leroux@hotmail.com